CW00790732

THE DOCKYARD, CHATHAM.

the stonemason

first edition thus
L-13 of clerkenwell, 2011

style: file under 'social history/fiction'

the stonemason

draft edition, for publick consideration.

original revelations - lived and imagined

by 'chyldish'

made public under oath.

the assembeled poem illustrating, skiving
and sketches made during a winter sojourn
in her majisys dockyard, c - in the year
1976.

to the publick

    yes, in this modern day and age a
secondary skool boy without qualifications
could consivably become a riter, but
he must 1st learn to rite like an old
woman then craft his fucking prose like
a hiddious lace doyly, for surving up
overly sugery angel cake, then drooping
it over the face of the dead.

              signed, gustov claudius

do not desire the glitter of jewel
but the raw roughness of stone

                    tao te ching

the cow field was vailed in mist. down
the hill comes a young man wearing a
victorian military jacket. he vaults the
style and disappears into the vapour.

it is as if the cows low in welcome,
before they too are swallowed into the
ground.

when an author says ground, he means
the general feeling of land, sky and
animel being made one.

ive got my scarlet colour-sergeants
jacket on. it is a little on the tight
side, due to all the people who populated
that age being midgits. upon the arm are
3 splended bullion stripes, above which
sits the emblem of 2 crossed flags and
on the cuff, the 2 crossed rifels of a
marksman, and a queens crown.

this perfict attire - if someone
wants to be conspicqious - cost me 3
pounds, bought from masons antique shop
on jeffery street, g -.

walking thru the cows field i aim for
the mists of time, then catch the bus to
m -.

actually, lets stay in this misty
cows field a moment longer. you can see
the dew sparkling on the grass and as
you come up the hill, the thrusting sun

making a halo effect. also, rising into
the sky you spy fort h -. now the mist
is burning off and little by little the
world is revealing itself in its god-like
glory. the fort is a mound really, hidden
benith a blanket of a thousand hawthorn
bushes. ive shinneyed down a tree into
the ditch there, then scailed the other
side clinging to the twigs of a sicamore;
30 feet up holding on by the tips of my
toes and 2 finger nails. really, thats all
that saved me: clinging to the concreat.

once inside the fort i crawled on my
belly between those hawthorns. there are
myrad tunnels twisting and turning benith
the brambels. a great entrence tunnel
also lies benith one hillock. there
criminals do up bent motors. you see them
in their masks and overalls - doing re-
sprays and switching number plates.

as that fort rises up in front of
you, you imagin machine guns and all
manner of exciting war stores stuffed
down those tunnels: hidden stuff, when in
reality its just chock full of old tyers
and rusting car bumpers.

but thats all ancient history.

breathing hard from climbing the
hill with my extra quick walking, i vault
the style at the top and take a quick
rest. on the right the old dew pond with
its dirty looking ducks waddling in the
mud, up ahead, the main road.

i head off again.

you can see cows hoof marks heading
to the muddy bank of the pond from where
they come to drink in the mornings and
evenings. every passing day the mud gets
more and the water gets less and less.
and when its all gone, then what?

theres still a farm house standing
over there. thou it dosnt look much, its
the last one left round these parts, all
the others have gone west. after this
field its just houses, houses and houses.

a green double decker comes round
the bend so sticking my arm out i trot
to the bus stop and jump on board. my
scarlet jacket startles the driver, who
sits there at the wheel in his peaked hat
with a fag on the go.

i like stamping my feet as i go up
the metal stairs.

from up top you can see rite across
the old air field. the giant hangers
stand out there all empity and felorn.
they built the stirling bombers in those
during the war - they'er the ones with
the giant undercarrages.

behind the hangers is another little
hill of hawthorn bushes with its hidden
counter-scarp tunnels.

when the conductor comes i get
away with paying 1/2 fair and sit there
examining the incomprehesable purple
printing on my greenish ticket. the paper
is soft and dusty feeling. if you taste

it, it sucks the spit out your mouth
like blotting paper. i love bus tickets,
and cinema tickets. the old style cinema
tickets are arguably the best with their
pinkish colour.

at the top of the downs we pass
over the motorway and then one more step
down hill and heres the wield, stretching
away flat as you like; the silver worm of
the river, sparkling in the distence and
little puffs of smoke going up from the
paper mills.

yes, i am in love with the world
of uniforms, caps and tickets. also the
machines that issue them, with their neat
little fold-out handels, are a delite
to the sences. when the world of cute
clockwerk machines finnaly passes, which
they assure us will be soon, the world
will be a sadder and shittyer place.

the purpose of my journy is to visit
the r - w - k - regimental museum.

over c - way the river is salty,
here it is young and tame and fresh.
this is where i went fishing as a young
skool boy and caught a jack-pike. quite
near the locks, actually. on this side
of the lockages its tidel and brackish,
on the m - side you get gudgeons and
sticklebacks.

i look down on the gateway of the
old barracks as we come into town. theres
a butifull nissan hut sat there, and you
can just make out the old regimental

officers mess with its white clap-board,
showing up thru the trees.

next its the white stone and flint
walls of the prison and its time to
jump off. about a mile up the back is
the heath where they used to hang us
criminals in our previous lives.

from here, the river is out of site
behind the hill. tuesdays theres a market
down by the bridge, where you can pick
up old cap badges and medals on the junk
stalls.

the museum is free.

i step up the pathway and in thru
the porch.

there in, a retired gentleman
officer, stood overly close to me.

these moments are apparently the
last days of my carefree life. yes, it is
time to stop being a skool boy and step
out into 'the big, bad world'.

the gentleman officer is showing me a
silver campaine medel with the egypt bar,
which he clasps in his yellow claw.

i look down on him: a tiny figure
wearing a cardigan and bandi legs incased
in karki, whipcord breeches. as a youth,
it is embarassing to suddenly have grown
taller than certen man of authority, to
have 'shot up' as it were.

this is not the 1st time that this

tiny curator has askt me into his office
and introduced me to his female secutary.
again she looks up at me from behind her
desk piled high with papers and surveys
me knowingingly thru her cat-eyed reading
glasses; again her face is painted up
like a pantomime dame; again she smiles
posionously before returning to her
typing machine.

no, i am not the 1st boy, one
presumes, to have been led 'back stage'
by this diminuative cavalry officer come
curator, to be guided down the narrow
corridoors that run behind the exhibits
- like some infernal rabbit warren - and
have had anceint draws slid open for ones
inspection then been invited to fondle
the medals of past heros of that nobel
regiment.

it is also entirely feasable
that the young man with soft bum fluth
sprouting from his plump red face - who i
previously saw blushing in the corridor
out side the curators office - was also
made to stand behind the said officer as
he bent himself over a chair and thrust
his boney whipcord-clad buttocks into the
youths groin area.

what draws this small, sparsly
haired, bispecticeld ex-officer, equwipt
with such thin bandy legs, yellow teeth
and finnly clippt mustasches to desire
me? he fumbles with my trousers but
his arthritic fingers cant undo my belt
buckle.

the spit drys up in my mouth and
im bearly breathing. i look down as
his knobley old knuckels fidgit with my
trousers. have these same fingers really
handled a cavalry carbine and sqeezed the
trigger, thus blowing a fuzzy-wuzzies
head clean off?

one thing is for certain: this
officers days of murdering black men are
well and truly hidden behind the vail.

its then that our little curator
emits a sudden cry of frustration, turns,
grasps the back of his chair and starts
thrusting himself back at me. all the
while he reaches behind, pulling at my
sleeves, trying to induce me to grasp his
old nags hips and sort him out.

it is wonderful to visit history, to
have such facilitys on ones doorstep.

also in the museum, they have
fish tanks with real live fish and bits
of pondweed floating about, creating
netwerks, islands and all round
underwater metropolises, for the snails
to crawl about in. and rite thru the
ajoinig doorway theres a whole gallery
full of stuffed birds.

and everything smells of wood and
dust and wax polish and scearsly a soul
enters whilest your gazing at the mothy
face of the last buzzud that dared air
its feathers over the skys of m -. and
the little brass inscription crows the
proud name of the idiotic member of

parlement who blasted it out the skys on august the 16th, 1864.

just out in the corridor lies a back staircase which leads you thru yet more dingy galleys.

here is piled an interesting heap of rusting farming impliments saved from a kentish barn by a fool, whilest over the grand fireplace hangs a busted shield and some pikes used to spear fellow englishmen during the civel war. next a row of glass display cases contain a hoard of chipped maniquins, who have been thrust into ill fitting jackets and lace up victorian boots and stair out at you like the memberes of some effernal interview panel, casting judgment as to weather or not you measure up for a job that nobody else wants and to all intents and purposes went out with the ark.

the whole effect is inhanced by a china faced doll with tuffts of real hair inserted in its scull - which grimices from the jaws of an ancient prambulator, offering conclusive proof that man is pursued and possessed by demons.

i decend by another staircase and stand directly oppersite the tall wooden door with 'curator' ritten upon it in gold leaf, i meet a life sized statue of a rearing horse carved in wite marble.

apart from distent voices coming in scattered snatches from other parts of the building there is a dusty silence.

looking benieth the horses uprised tail
is modelled its equine arse and cunt.

this was what i was enthralled by:
this is what my officer caught me fertivly
examining as he trotted out of his office
on his little bent pins.

quickly i take my hands away from
that rude part of the horse and stair
down at the horses left back hock. the
curator stands there motionless. i feel
his eyes burning into me until im forced
to look up. sternly he bekons to me,
whilest backing into his doorway. so i am
drawn into his dark world of sin.

history tells us that our bronse
age fore fathers had sex with horses.
the author imagins that he must have
once been just such a warrior, otherwise
why, for one still young, have i the
inclination to peer under the tail of a
marble horse?

i have signed my name to this page
so now it is impossible to pass myself
off as pure. thou of course i am.

that proud marble horse had
deeply defined buttocks, but what of my
shrivelled little officer? who can tell?

. . . so he thrusts his whipcord
clad nags bones back at my young loins,
and likewise tries to induce me to thrust
at him. but i could do no such thing and
just stood there in the dim lite, quite
frozen really.

repeatedly he reaches back and
places my hands on his narrow haunches
but each time he lets them go and re-
grasps the back of his chair i let my
hands fall to my sides again. in just
such a way i convay a compleat lack of
infusiasim for his gallant military life
of sodomy.

*   *   *

all in all it was impossible for me to
get excited at the prospect of having
sex with such a decaying, miniture,
imaciated, cavalry horse. even for the
prize of a nile campain medal with egypt
bar.

in memory of mrs john foad and her son
fred

dressed all in white a black man came
walking up the terraced streets that lead
from c - station. he walks with ease,
unaffraide of the hard pincht faces that
turn and grimice after him as he strolls
by in his flowing african robes.

what is such a man doing walking
in these unwelcoming streets? there are
plenty of indians and pakistanis in our
dismel towns, but a black man? no, west
indians and africans hardly ever show
there faces here, lest of all dressed in
robes.

it is true that rupurt is a champion
boxer. also of note is he is a master and
teacher of tie chi chaun and kung fu, but
still . . .

im sat on my big brothers racing
bike, leaning up against the wall of the
old community hall. on account of the
bike still being a little too high for me
i have one foot resting on the foundation
stone, which reads: in memory of mrs john
foad and her son fred.

other students are also awaighting
rupurt.

a smooth, with carfully blow-dryed
blond hair, stands hand in hand with his
feoncay, and talks with dylan, an indian
boy about my age, and already sporting a
silky looking mustache. but they are all
stood down in the little court yard by
the double green doors.

fools! you are blind to the world
down there, where-as from up here, i
can see clear down the street with my
excilent eyes.

rupurt grows from a speck in the
distence to full size, his teeth and eyes
smiling in his black face.

looking at him drifting along the
street like that, you cant help but think
that some desert nomade has come to show
us the path to a secret gardan oasis. it
is as if his feet arnt really walking up
paget street at all but are more like
gliding over the filthy paving slabs, and
so rupurts demina betrays no fear.

of course the community halls been
burned down since, but back then it was
our practice hall and we'ed troop in
there on wednesday nites and learn sticky
hand, taoist yoga, tie chi and wushu
kung-fu.

rupurt smiles and nods as he comes
up level, then i watch him shrink again
as he steps down the side of the hill to
pick up the keys off mrs baker.

the girl with large veluptious

breasts moving inside her mohire jumper
comes out of the terraced house oppersit,
leading her little brother by the hand. i
say hello then look away. of course she
smiles at me.

    i take my foot off of mrs john
foad and her son freds foundation stone,
balance there for a second, then slip
down off the hard leather racing sadle
and stand perched on my tippy toes, the
cold cross bar jammed up my cradock.

    what a thing these girls are:
walking about with their bodies; dressing
up in gaily coloured jumpers; smiling at
15 year old boys on racing bikes; and all
as if they feel that they are somehow
separate and not one of my possesions.
which of course they are not.

    theres the sound of a real motor
bike coming down the road and i crank my
head and peer up hill, along the line of
the rising asphelt. its the same feeling
as when you here an old hurrican or
spitfire going over: its voice tells you
that its not a man made machine going
over but somehow a living, breathing
creature, and commands you rush out and
peer into the skys.

    the more i look the more i can see
him coming: old cyclops banging along on
his triumph tiger.

    he pulls up, lifts his goggles
and survays us, the engin still gunning
away between his thighs. thats when you

see his face is all mashed up. one of
his cheeks is all caved in and his rite
eye is nesteled down there next to his
nostrel. maybe cyclops was attacket with
a hammer as a small child, or perhaps he
slipped from his bike and fell under a
tram. plus the bridge of his nose isn't
quite there anymore, as if the bones have
softened up and kind of flattend out,
apart from the tip which sticks out in a
little bobble. in truth it would be rong
to say that he has a nose at all.

cyclops lets the engin die, waddels
his bike down into the little court yard,
then manfully hoists it up onto its
stand.

i, in turn, hook my leg over the
crossbar of my bike, pat the handel bars,
where a horse would have his head and
feed it a lump of sugar. i then walk my
bike over and say hello to cyclops. only
i dont address him as cyclops on account
that his real name is graham.

graham comes all the way down from l
- on his motor bike to assist rupurt with
the lesons.

yes, cyclops is a good few grades
up from us novises, because old cyclops's
cantonese jacket is a distinct turqoise
colour, which he rubs in our face as he
pidgions about the practice hall, puffing
his chest out this way and that. that
gaudy jacket is proof that he has taken
his 4th grade and he nods and springs

24

into action when ever rupurt scruntches
his brow. you could legitamitly say that
cyclops is at rupurt's beck and call.

us novises wear orange ribons that
bearly show against the yellow of our
jackets. actually, im permited to wear a
green ribbon but i have not had it sewn
to my breast as i for one choose not to
strut about flinging my acomplishments in
peoples faces.

i can tell that graham dosnt like me
because he dosnt respond to my cheerfull
greating and instead mearly squints
his damaged lower eye at me. not that
i really dare look into it. most males
in authority have a problem with my
existence and why should this disfigured
example be an exception? i of course show
double kindness towards him, and have in
fact made a drawing of lau-tzu, which i
will present to him at the appropriat
time. will he then still view me as the
enemy?

enemy is perhaps too strong a
word. maybe bored indiffrence to a
fledgling subordinant would be a truer
feeling. or is cyclops simply jellouse
of my compleat face? or is it becouse im
unbound and cear free? certenly graham
imagins himself highly advanced and grown
up. that little lower eye is watery and
reddened. actually both his eyes are
blue/gray in colour, not unlike a pair of
sad oysters sitting in pink juce.

my drawing of lau-tzu has been
executed in pen and ink. the little china
man can be seen riding on his donky and
smirking away to himself as a carving of
a taoist lion sits looking blindly on.

have i made this picture to entice
cyclops in to liking me? very probably.
but also, to make him and the others
see that i too am special, that i am an
artist, that i am kind and a cut above
the other run of the mill students.

really it is to grow in rupurts
estermation.

when rupurt calls you out front
to illustrate a move, you cant help but
notice the most unussual scent on his
palms as they push past your chin.

the drawing is rolled up in my old
army haversack, along with my plimpsols
and bottle of ginger beer.

is it rong to judge people simply
on their outward apperences? of course it
is. that is why i have made it my quest
to make graham like me.

rupurt comes back up the hill
holding the bunch of keys and unlocks
the doors. i waight for everybody else
to go in 1st, which is only good manners,
then follow in last wheeling my push bike
across the wooden floor boards. looking
at them filing in before me, i wonder if
these people even know anything about
the werks of van gogh, salvador dali,

francis bacon, andy warhole, rothco,
jimi hendrix, the napoleonic navi and
the history of the m - forts. it seams
doubtfull.

*   *   *

the men get changed in a little side
room, cluttered with boxes full of old
junk: mothy curtens mostly, plus some
lampshades and a string of bunting from
the days of the empire. the girls,
there's only 2 of them, get changed in
the toilets.

    rupurt pulls his desert robes over
his head and i see his hard black body
before he dresses in his masters costume,
which is silky black with yellow trim.

    when we'er in uniform, as it were,
we have to stand and bow before we enter
the practice hall. for this you put your
rite fist in the palm of your left hand
and nod your head. this symbolises that
we are here to practice, not to punch
each others lites out.

    the smooth, his clown fieonsay,
dylan, veluptious breast, and her little
brother, and me, all line up on one side
of the hall and rupurt stands out front
and leads us thru our stretching and
warming up exercises. of course cyclops
is also stood out front, only slightly

to the side so that those who cant get
a clear view of rupurt can whatch him
instead.

naturally graham is a great example
to us novises. he always follows rupurts
instructions most maticliously, and never
fails to be beaten into submission when
ever rupurt needs to demonstrate how to
fend off an idotic attacker. in a strange
way i begin to ignore rupurt altogether
and instead focus on grahams strange
face and rather brittle interpritations
of what is in fact ment to be a flowing,
magical dance.

of course it is rong to mentally
dissect an indervidul, because no matter
how virtuios the subject, one inverably
finds them guilty of every vice. so i
refuse to make such negitive observation
and instead concentrate on the positive
aspects of grahams intepretation. no
doubt if id paid more attention at skool
and honed my mind, i would be able to
learn many important 'wrinkels' from this
unussual creature.

and after all, graham is not here at
the behest of some wandering freek show,
for us to gawp at, and ridicule like
village idiots, but is offering us the
benefit of years of dogged obsevence. no,
it is not for nothing that graham wears a
glowing, colbolt blue ribbion emblazoned
across his breast.

so i put away any petty comparisons

and allow myself to follow each subtle
gesture of his genuinely expressive
hands. and if graham is destroying poetry
with every thrust, so to speak, then i
can turn my attention to rupurt and copy
each stance as it is executed in the
manner of a ballet, thus this ancient
form is transmuted down the generations
and committed to memory.

although it is against the whole
ethos of this dissaplin, i cant help but
occassionaly look around the room and
compair myself to otheres. and where ever
i throw my eyes i am confronted by a pair
of veluptious thrusting breasts.

as we go into stork pose, i force
my eyes from the outline of a very large
and puffy nipple and instead stair up at
the rafters. there are bear lite bulbs
hanging there.

when we turn and exicute lunge - the
dragon - i narrow my eyes. even from
behind it is possible to see the edges
of her breasts protruding from under her
arm. quickly, i look away and examin the
home made curtens that are hanging in
all the little windows. they are quite
on the thin side, have prints of vintage
motorcars on them, and some would say
let in too much lite to forñll their
function.

up the end of the hall, above the
tiny stage, is an old faded print of the
queen hanging lopsided.

the more i bite down and try to
consentrate, the more my eyes demand to
entertain themselves, ogling 1st her leg
and then her ear lobe.

rupurt instructs us to pair off to
practice sticky hand. me and veluptious
breasts hang back, so's that we are the
last ones left and become partners by
defult.

in sticky hand you face each other
with your feet stepped a pace apart, and
the backs of your right hands touching.
you then have to remain in contact
with each other whilest you sway in
the breese, trying to distablize your
opponint. naturally we look into each
others eyes, and we both smile and look
away.

next we have to practice our fighting
pattens.

we are told to gather round rupurt
as he takes us thru some tricky evasions.
he instructs cyclops to attack him.
cyclops steps into dragon and strikes,
if the truth is to be told, somewhat in
slow motion. rupurt deftly side steps and
with the tinyist of shoves sends cyclops
reeling across the room.

cyclops brushes himself down and
springs back over to rupurt like a happy
dog. rupurt waights a moment, gathers
himself then nods for cyclops to attempt
another attack.

this time rupurt mearly swings
his shoulder, pulls litely on cyclops
rist and cyclops carrys on going, flying
forward, tripping over his own feet, then
crashing to the floor.

this time cyclops picks himself up
a little more slowly, then limps over and
bows deeply in front of rupurt.

now rupurt goes thru the patten in
slow motion, bit by bit, so's we get the
hang of it. cyclops stands obediently,
awaights his cue. rupurt gives him the
sign to step in and supprisingly, cyclops
is again expertly out witted.

finnaly rupurt asks the girl with
the veluptious breasts to tie a blindfold
over his eyes. again he instruckts
cyclops to attack him. cylops circles
him, keeping just out of range, then
makes a faint to the left before rushing
in. rupurt immediately sences the attack,
redirects cyclops's blow, plonks him on
his bum and stands over him with 2 fingers
poised over cyclops eyes.

we novis's stand in a circle looking
down at cyclops laid flat out on his back
between rupurts legs. every time he so
much as breaths, rupurt applys a rist
lock that forces cyclops to emit a small
whimper.

of couse, if you really were attact
by cyclops youed have to do your fingers
pritty wonky, as his arnt strickly on the
level.

"i sence his auroa so i know his intent, and therefore where his energy is directed. and where his energy is directed, i help him go." explains rupurt.

dylan puts his hand up. "what if hes got a knife?"

i catch the eye of veluptious breasts and we both smerk at this patently silly question.

"if you were ever so unlucky as to be attackt with any weapon, the safist option is to run," states rupurt, gravely. "actually always run, if you can."

dylan looks pretty disgusted with this answer. "but that just shows your chicken." he declairs angrily.

rupurt looks at him closely. "chicken?"

"yeah, chicken. you know, sceardy cat." and dylan looks around the room for support, but we all look down.

"it is best to avoid all violence, if possible." says rupurt leavely.

cyclops nods at us viggeriously, before again crying out in pain and beating the floor with his free hand as rupurt applys pressure to his twisted rist.

dylans toung comes out and licks at

his dark, soft haired mustache. "yeah,
but couldn't you just poke his eyes out
and then snap his arm?"

releasing his grip, rupurt helps
cyclops from the floor boards and turns to
dylan. "listen, if you ever come face to
face with a street fighter, just run."

we all look at rupurts face to see
if he's joking.

"im not joking. even if they are
unarmed, run. a street fighter will
always win in a straight fight because
he dosnt care if he kills you. he has
no restraint. im a boxer, but i wouldn't
like to take on a street fighter. you only
stand and fight if you have to. now lets
get back in line."

we turn and walk back to our places.
dylan sidels past me, "whats the point of
learning all this shit if we'er not going
to stand and fight!" i smile as if i agree
with him.

last off we do some tie chi paterns
and practice glueing our selve's to the
floor by sinking our chi and then its
meditation: basicly that involves sitting
and breathing into our tummys, just
bellow our belly buttons.

rite after we finish rupurt has
to leave to get the train back up the
smoke. he pulls his robes on over his
uniform and we bow to him as he waves and
rushes out. as we go into the changing

room we have to turn and bow again to
the practice room, as we are still in
uniform.

graham is left in charge of locking
up and returning the keys.

the 1st thing i do befor getting
changed is open my bottle of ginger beer.
i take a swig, then hand cyclops the
rolled up drawing ive made for him. i
turn and start unlacing my plimpsoles.

from the corner of my eye i can
see cyclops examining my carefully made
studdy. his head nods thortfully, his
hand comes up and his fingers toy with
the sparse line of ginger bristles that
battle to obscure a pink scar running
across his upper lip.

i bang my plimpsoles together and
stuff them down the side of my haversack.
graham turns and looks across at me. i
pick up my bottle of ginger beer and take
another vicious swig at it, accidently
bashing my teeth on the bottle top. the
sweetness rushes into my mouth and i open
my kneck and pour away. theres a sudden
cutting pain in my guts and i groan and
crease up.

"thank you for showing me the
drawing." i look up. old cyclops is
trying to give me back my drawing.

"no its for you." i wince.

"for me?"

"yes."

"where did you get it."

"i drew it," i say, holding onto my guts.

"you drew this?"

"yes."

"its remarkable." and he trys to hand it to me again.

"no, its for you."

"for me?"

"yes . . . a gift."

"thank you. thank you very much. ile have to show rupurt, your very talented."

ah, yes. that is true, i am very talented. but after all, isn't art just another trick, like everything else? you learn to do it and then it isn't very difficult at all, but the morons are impressed.

"thats quite allrite," i gasp, "im glad you like it." i turn and sink down onto a chair. really, now i think of it, i should have given him the drawing in front of the girls. after all, isn't the whole point of art to impress women into loving you?

"so you've read the tao te chin?"

"yes," i nod.

35

"how old are you?"

"16 on the 1ˢᵗ of december."

"you should come to 1 - and train. this," and he looks about the shabby store cupboard, "is a very good introduction, rupurt is a wonderfull teacher but you need to meet professor chee soo."

i shrug.

"you dont know who chee soo is? really? a truly amazing man. he is rupurts master. chee soo was a tank commander during the last war, won the military medal, was captured by the japanease in burma then escapped over the mountains with a couple of other escapease. they were living in the jungels, off fruets, snakes and insects for over 6 months."

i try to focus on what cyclops is saying. theres a real tearing sensation in my guts.

"sorry, where did you say he teaches?"

"e - court."

"but then i have to get up to 1 -."

"yes, but there is a regular train survis."

"ile have to see if i can afford it."

"dont worry, if your ment to come it will happen. proffesor chee soo says to never put effort into anything. theres no need to look into booking a holliday in bemudah because if your ment to go on holliday to bemudah then the broucher and booking form will come thru the post."

"really, what about madigasca?"

"absolutely."

"they have caeleocamphs in madigasca."

"the world will give you what you need, not what you want. ying and yang, a little of each in the other. if your in harmony with the way then there is no conflict. the lowest thing on earth is water, but it is also the strongest."

i nod my head. "if i get my apprenticship in the dockyard i mite have to go to l -, to do my city and guilds."

"well there you are then. thats your opportunity. think about it, you mite be suprized by what you learn." and cyclops looks at me mysteriously.

"how do you mean?" i have to let out a burp.

"excuse me."

cyclops looks at me pittyingly. "i mean his name, chee soo, for a start. have you thort about it?"

i try thinking about it. "no, not really."

"chee soo. thats 2 silabuls. dose it remind you of anybody elese?" and he lets his smaller eye, the one nestled in his cheek, rove all over me and then blink. for some strange reason i have to think of the eye of a spurm whale peering out of that great blunt head. i shrug.

"chee - soo, je - sus." anouciates cyclops, and then folds his arms and allows his lower lips to pucker out. "dont you see? its too close for it to be a coinsdence. chee - soo, je - sus!"

"mmm, i see what you mean." i say vagely, looking 1st at his regular eye, then oppting to take a last swig on my ginger beer.

"you know you shouldn't be drinking that stuff. its just sugar water."

"its ginger beer." i correct him.

"yes, and 90 percent sugar. you know the most evil company in the world? tate and lyle. white sugar = white death!"

i grit my teeth and nod. actually the pain is passing.

"i just got thirsty, thats all."

"thats the chi burning up the impurities within the body. if you must drink, drink plane tap water, but better still, drink nothing. look at me, i dont

drink. im shrinking my kiddnys to the
size of chestnuts. one small cup of warm
water in the mornings, thats all. nothing
else passes my lips all day, not even
tea."

and he turns proudly to the room.

"my kiddnys must be like cockels
by now," he announces, and he holds his
thumb and index finger out as if squeezing
a grape. every one is caught, stood half
naked. "remember, we are what we eat."
adds cyclops, he nods sagely, before
turning to me again. "looking at our
friend here i presume he eats a lot of
chicken."

they all peer at me with renewed
interest, assessing wether i look like a
chicken or not.

i dress quickly and throw my
haversack over my shoulder.

"im off then."

"yes, thanks for the drawing."

"your welcome."

i grab my bike and wheel it out of
the practice hall. one can only presume
that cyclops eats a diet consisting
mainly of scrambled eggs.

chapter 3

an interview

the room was smoky. 3 men, sat behind
a long oaken desk face the candidete,
puffing away on their snouts with only one
ashe tray between the lot of them.

in a way it seamed that their
very faces - and of course their almost
puppet-like heads - danced in and out of
the swirles of bitter tobacco smoke.

the whole world was smokey back
then, or so it seamed.

and the windows were shut tight,
keeping out the fresh air of spring and
any chance of the sun aluminating the
gloom.

of course, sun lite is not kept out
by mear windows, but this was the effect,
or should we say feeling.

it seams strange to be sat here -
facing these gray faces - being assessed
for abiltys that i most certenly lack.
and all-the-while nodding and smiling at
their words, as if i agree with them, or
we shear some subtle joke about the irony
of existence; or as if i understand what
on earth they are talking about; or as if
i am the correct person for their gastly
aprentiship and can do maths, geomitary

and spelling, and all sorts of crazy
sumersalts that you must learn in skool
and 'apply yourself too' or simply fail
in life.

but i never did and now its too
late.

and all the while they grumble on
and i gaze thru the smoke at the lappels
of one with a ginger comb-over, who is
wearing a demob suit from the age of my
grandfather.

those lapells really are dusted to
the hilt with dandruff, looking for all
the world like the sloaps of some strange
snowy mountain top.

ginger comb-over asks another
question and i nod, supplying the
impression of keenness coupeled with
correct thinking.

also, his fingers are buitifully
nicotine stained and the edges of his
graying tash dangle there - over his thin
ginger lips - like a net curtain gone
mouldy. then his teeth, neat and yellow,
peeking thru, like little men peering
thru a waterfall.

its easy to gaze at the world
and just see the colours and mirage of
existence and forget the rigours and
underlying structure and the nessesitys
of employment.

the 1st thing is to be an artist.

the 2nd is to be great and true.

the 3rd is to grow in estermation.

the 4th is to smash the enimys and win.

the 5th is to become holyer than jesus.

or should we say that failer is the greatist success?

yes, i love to invert the truth; to stand facts on their head and force them to reveal their tretchery. after all, isnt this the true test of truth.

as it happens im basicly here to please my mother, who is intent on my 'toeing the line'. yes, thats why im sat in front of these ancient judges: to finnaly face the facts of life.

and my father? thats another matter.

but the very notion of one of his tadpoles returning, as it were, to the primevil pool of the dockyards? why, he'd have a blue fit. or rather, he'd piss in the wardrobe, fall over drunk and do nothing.

naturally a young fellows instinct is to become a hero, but thats not always an option for a skool boy. it saems that if i truly followed my hart - and gods path - it would quite swiftly end with getting my teeth kicked in, and back out again, for an onchor.

it seams that the world is ruled
by liers and the fakers, mostly. by the
bullys and the yes men, in general. by
my perents and my big brother, old nick,
really. and by my teachers, mainly. and
as my mother always says 'its best not to
voice oppinions or contradict people'.

but arnt these judges the very ones
who give inserection its butiful form?

back to my big brother, old nick. he
at least will be happy that im following
in our grandfathers footprints, because
old nick knows that i will be hobbeled by
life and will no longer pose a threat to
his specialness.

yes indeed, my brother is an artist.

or at least has asperations. to
be plain, he is a student in our great
capitol, studdying at one of our finer
instituions.

do you know something? old nick
did a perfict illustration of a boot, a
still life they call it. he drew in the
laces, the lace-holes, the stiching,
then shaded it all in quite dutifully.
then this tutor comes up behind him, and
with a great big brush paints rite over
old nicks meticlious pencil study with 3
viloent slashes.

"that is a boot!" announcs the
tutor.

quite hellerious stuff. being a

nice gramer skool boy old nick was a bit
schocked.

john hoyland was the name of that
mighty tutor stood over him with a
dripping paint brush in hand, and some
sort of fierce beared, i imagin.

＊　　　　　　＊　　　　　　＊

the clock on the wall clicks the 1/2
houre and comb-overs ciggeret lifts to
his mouth. at this hidden signel the
others also lift their fags to their dry
lips and take a deep drag, as one.

each tip is fevershly sucket into
life and another great ploom of smoke
goes up to the already nickotine stained
cealing.

1, 2, 3 and then the fags come to
rest again, each cigerets balancing on
the rim of the old bakerlite ashetray,
their owners sat there quite dead now.
no movement at all really, sleeping
puppets, only their hands lifting now and
again, scratching their hairy ears with
their pens. prehaps riting some note or
other across the papers that lie upon the
blotters infront of them.

did i tell you im not smoking? im
sat bolt upright in my chair, faceing my
interigators with an air of apprehension.

no ciggeret nor jockular pipe is
clentchet between my already ruined
teeth. in dumb insolence, really.

yes, sarcasam is etched across my
clean young face. and though i am timid,
i am also ready to dismiss this puppet
theater by maticlious observation of
their exaggerated features, comic faults
and many vices.

is it rong of me to mock? is it
possible that benith my exterior of
failed youth i too have an inflated
sence of my own specialness and am quite
prepaired to go and live out my dreams,
taking my lodgins in a cardboard box on
the streets if nessisary?

'no, i do not need your vile
appreticship, you gray bearded buffoons!'

thats my feeling in a nut shell.

becoming a tramp and taking to the
streets would certenly teach the world
a leason. and if i died of tuburclosis
because of it? well, that would meerly
underline the tragedy.

so you see my gay puppets, im
not the regular broken candidet, sent
hobbling from a secondary skool to crawl
before you like an abject begger, i am
gustov claudius, if my birth cirtifficet
is spelled correctly.

oh no, a job is not everything, by
any means.

fore instance, has it not occurred
to you gentleman of the panel, that i
might prehaps preffer to be an artist
like my big brother, old nick? that i too
mite wish to don a basque beret, rather
than a werking mans cloth cap, and speak
of great art rather than fart and spit
oysters for good queen bess.

becouse, thou i am ugly and have
been thus far shunned by the world of
women, with one gloryious exception,
i fully intend to use art to prove
my worth. rather than trudging under
dockyard crains in the drizzel i will be
held in the arms of a naked model and
be fed fresh milk from her missile like
breasts. milk gushing over my chin.

and then to grasp her muscular flanks
and leave my colbolt thumb prints, rite
there on her piss flaps.

yet here i sit trapped before you,
motionless as it were, awaighting your
judgment and art and girls remain as
alien to me as happyness.

and life drawing in the hot studios
of the gifted? i am not welcome, i have
not been even invited. or to put it more
succinctly: i have been barred. yes, i
have offically been refused entry into
art skool on the grounds of my lack of
education and piss poor exame results.
essentually none.

so here i stand before you, esteamed
wooden heads, and i ask you to please

ignore any defect you may persive in my
mind and demina, and welcome me into the
world of werking men and nailed boots
with your open arms. in effect, im upon
my knees befor you. an outcast.

i saw your splendid advert in the
local, and the postion advertised seamed
appealing to me in its way. will the job
ever live up to my expectations? who can
say? thou it seams frankly doubtfull. but
so is my lot: to scrape for aceptence,
this situation forced upon me by certain
predicaments.

predicaments! theres a word. a
sarcastic hook if you will. a vilinious
deployment, infused with dirty meanings.

i use it here not to add lite to
my poem, but to drag the listner down
to my level. you see i will stoop to any
depths, even riting begging letters.
that, im afraid, is the nature of poets.
yes, ive ritten you an essay on my
meny faults and attributes. yet riting
irritates me - in that sence im a lao tzu
- at skool i could scearsly fill half a
page. but here i must give good account
so's i can gain a station in life.

can you picture that: outside
the skool window the trees seam to be
calling out to me, beckoning in the rainy
cold distence, with their damp, knobbly
twigs.

jays, robins, blue tits and the
sudden wren, all are asking me to escape

47

and return to the woods. at these times
the skool boy imagins himself to be an
artist, thrusting thru that undergrowth,
dragging spoiled canvases behind him; on
his way home to his model girlfriend, to
be fed his warm breast milk supper.

but no matter how you catorgerize
these 'wild feelings' - it is best for me
to just admit that they are trembling and
un-met and that i am never to become an
artist. so in effect i am yours!

lets just say that i have a skool
boys desires that are closer to dreams.

not that i dont see that you
gentleman of the pannel are nothing
but a mirage of the moment; even your
supposedly solid heads and mighty oaken
desk is but stardust waiting to viberate
away into nothingness.

yes, i am fit for the job at hand.

yes, i am trustworthy.

yes, i am the young man you are
looking for.

what else can i tell you?

what would you like to here? that i
will be a slave to your job and will werk
in all weathers for pennys?

and with this perception of myself
as lowly and less, am i not the most
virtuious of underlings?

have no fear, it seams certain that
these 'wild feelings' will never be met
and that as an adult i shall be alone and
ugly. of this much my mother, and my big
brother, old nick, have assured me.

worn out by years of toil in your
survis, without a paint brush in sight, i
will reamain forever humbeled, gratfull
and indebted to you, the woodenheaded
gentlemen of the panel, for the gift of
this 'postion'.

of course my father, thou absent,
also predicts my ruination and ultimate
missery.

then this is how i have been
prepaired for employment: with threats,
blows and damning predictions.

so why dose art allude me and not
my big brother, old nick? why is it he
who is poised to take his postion in art
and life whilest i am forced to beg on my
knees for a position in a trade that all
but died out in the middle ages?

gentleman of the pannel, i
must respectfully ask how, with good
conchions, you can take a young
impressionable lad, myself in this case,
under your wing as it were, when you know
in your wood wormed old harts that this
so called job of yours is an empty sham,
and that this apprentiship, which i am
begging for, holds no prospects what-
so-ever, and worse than all of this,
prommises no poerty.

whilest old nick makes ridiclious
doodles of boots that are mocked and
defaced by bored and hoary faced art
tutors, i have to sit here on my hands
and whatch old men nod and doze whilest
pretending to asess my metal thru a cloud
of posionious smoke.

it seams that old nick has
been rewarded for his obedience and
gargantchewen brain, whilest i have been
rewarded for my scearcrows head, which
apparently no type of education could
have helpt.

thats actually quite funny: i have a
scearcrows head and the inquistion before
me have puppet heads.

the clock on the wall ticks and
another moment passes.

all 3 lite fresh blue lines, puff
and take sips of dusty water from the
tumbers lined in front of them.

"so," says comb-over, "you were
educated at such and such a skool?"

"yes" i beam helpfully.

he looks at me, his head cocked on
the end of its string. it really is as if
his eyes have been painted on by the hand
of a child.

'education', thats another word
people throw about like a sledge hammer.
a word contaning one hundred blows and

then some add-ons.

i realise that i may have over
stated my resivations previolsly, and
that one must conceed that freedom is to
be found thru the love of honest hard
labour.

foremost, a youth is formed into a
man by obedience and a love of dissaplin.
and you can add belieth onto that.

some hot heads may argue that such
obedience is wrung from a curtailment of
a chylds verve and wit. there is no doubt
that those who hammer disaplin into the
brains of the young reveal nothing but
their own deep rooted fear of life.

thats another meaning to that
special word: curtailment. yes, education
is a conspiracy of endings and a haven
for those who enjoy the simulated
experence of thinking. no, not thinking,
they do have a form of thinking, rather a
simulated experence of imagination.

so they cling to a raft of idiotic
idears that is sucked into the swirling
maw of a charybdis.

here is the letter i rote on the
back page of my application form, listing
the reasons why any prospective employer
should engage me, and why i wish to
become an apprentice stonemason.

i have ritten it out in purple ink,
as at skool we were instruckted, very

firmly, to never rite such applications in
red.

to whom-so-ever it may concern:
reasons for engaging the excilent
applicant gustov claudius.

forward and forwarning.

natureally, 1st and foremost i wish
to become an artist. this dose not mean
that i nessiserally persive stone masonry
as being a meer craft, 7veral rungs
bellow me. on the contary, i can assure
the panel that i see stonemasonry as
elevated and far above and beyond me.

of course it will always be argued
that drawing and painting are the true
high arts. how else could a man invisage
a pyramid, for example, unless he 1st
imagined such a thing, then drew it
with a pencil? but dose that make stone
masonry lowly and subsevent? some would
say so.

it is also true that a pyramid, no
matter how high and grandious, is still
in effect nothing but a pile of ordered
rubble dreamed up in the artists mind,
then barrowed into a heap by a hoard of
lesser beings.

is that to harsh of me?

let us just supose that had the
art skool considered my application,
rather than dissmissng it out of hand
because i lack certain nessisary entry
qualifications, then i wouldn't be sat
here before you today, gentlmen, humbly
begging for a job that in all honesty is
benith my dignity to bow and scrape for.

isn't it better to be honest from
the outset rather than test your patents,
rather than mock your interlects, or
spout obvious lies?

on being approved for the above
postion of stonemasons apprentice,
i shall, despite these deeply felt
missgivings, endevour to do my duty and
'pull my waight' in all instance. for
i am young and viggerious and up for
anything.

but really, can any job be that
taxing? i doubt it.

again let us be honest gentlemen
- and i presume i am addressing myself to
gentlemen - does any one of you really
'pull your waight'? i think the answer to
this question would be a resounding no.
even our prime minister, one presumes,
loafs about all day pressing his plump
thighs against some conveiniant radiator.

so armed with the foreknowlage
that even you, my betters, are weak,
lazy and shy of hard graft, it seams
to run against the grain to expect me,
a meer begginer in life, as it were -

who by definition is easerly decived by
the ways of the 'grown up world' - to
show infusiasm, or know the coads and
protocols of gaining gamefull employment.

how could i, as a greenhorn, be
privey to such esoteric knowllege? of
course im not. it would be rediclious!

besides, if these archeic 'coads'
and 'proticols' of employment still exist
in the modern world, which it seams very
possibly they do, then isn't it the duty
of the young to shun and smash them?

it seams fairly obvious that
mentally, phisicaly and spiritually, man
has been in decline since the advent of
farming and the subsequent ingestion of
poisions in the form of weat glueten.
with this knowllege in mind i submit
that it is not the intention of this
prospective canidate to take advantage,
or judge his futcher employers to
harshly.

isn't it interesting how only a
pidgion, or perhaps a house sparrow, is
eqwipt with a digestive tract to deal
with grains?

know wonder that everyone is feeling
so lack-luster these days, and are mearly
going thru the motions of werk and
obedence. imagin a roman solder marching
for 18 hours a day, building his camp,
sleeping for 4 hours and then his off
again to conquior the britons.

yes, we have undermind our werk
force with cheep, inaporpreate foodstuffs
and as a race we are in genetic decline.

so i beg of you - when you know that
you yourselfs are in error - do not judge
me to haistyly. and if i am at 1st slow
and unable to comprehend orders, or am
late for werk due to excessive tiedness,
please indulge these weaknesses.

remember, the werking life is best
suited to a brainless idiot. im sure
that even the gentleman of the panel, if
i dare point the finger, could compleat
their weeks werk on monday morning and
spend the rest of the week lazing about
in bed, or visiting a bath house, or
pretend to be fishing by a conveiant
river. if, instead, you choose to keep
up this sham: pretending to be bissy,
whilest all along doodling fancifull
monsters and passing stacks of dusty,
moth-eaten old paper from one deptment to
the next, for no good reason other than
to passify some meaningless, ingrained
werk ethic that was passed to you like
a poisoned challis from some long dead
victorian who has since turned to dust or
gone damp with mildew, then that is your
look out ...

yes, im talking of the dockyard now.

some people will say that the life i
aspire to - that of an artist and student
- is in itself inderlent. that may be so,
but art is my calling.

yours sincerely

gustov claudious

ps

be assured that i will apply myself to
any task set before me with rigour and
dedication, regardless of my resservations
and preffrence for freedom.

chapter 4

reflections on an interview

yes, my big brother has had his
wings well and truly clipped and has
gone to live in the capitiol to 'become
someone'.

meanwhile i will drag my fresh young
body into the dockyard and doth my cap as
my grandfathers did before me.

the salty sea is calling out for
my family's blud, and its down to me to
shoulder the responsibility and bed down
under the dockside crains with convict
ghosts and ancient mariners. and then,
after many years servis, thru honest
toil, and by subduing certain wayward
instincts - no doubt related to my
artistic nature - i shall be imbewed with
a belith in myself sufficiently limited
to make my mother proud of me, and the
artists of the past weep.

that is, if the kind gentlemen of
the panel will view me with kindness and
compassion and throw me this stinking
prize.

some of that gentleman's dandruff
is actually fag ash and some of the fag
ash is actually dandruff, not sawdust. im
aluding to his puppet heritage again.

is it really so rong to make jokes

in poems? sarcasim and mockery are one
thing, but does that exclude love and
charity.

after all there are all sorts
of proticals to becoming someone in
ones chosen field. of course i am not
surgesting for one moment that i am cut
out for chipping stone for the rest of
my born natural, but could i not instead
become some sort of a poet living under a
rock? that would be highly amusing. like
a rain beetle with a quil, instead of
anteni.

in a democrracey even skool boys
from the w - secondary skool for boys
canot always be phisicly refrained from
putting their illiterate fances to paper.
perhaps this is the problem: democracy,
and now every rag-a-muffin can become an
artist.

but even if ive snatch't privlages
beyond my station, as it were, this dosnt
mean that i should embark on an open
day, taking the rise out of the delicate
sencibiltys of true essayists, and random
pot shots at aged puppet heads, dose it?

to get on in life, in art and
litrichar, one must curb ones baser
inclinations; limit ones hunger for wit,
truth and verve, and use the term 'one'
for talking about the self rather than
'me' or 'i'.

yes, in this modern day and
age a secondary skool boy without

qualifications could consivably become a riter, but he must 1st learn to rite like an old woman and craft his fucking prose like a hiddious lace doyly, for surving up overly sugery angel cake, then drooping it over the face of the dead.

my big brother, old nick would preffer it that i concentrated on my riting so as never to turn the god-like serch-lite of my hart to the painting of pictures, and thereby outshine him on the battle field of art. mark my words, i will become englands 1st true artist, thou my astranged father also requires me to never rise from the mire and challenge his weak artistic assperations.

so to the dockyard!

yes, forget art, i will embody a belieth in a life benieth the crains and beside the great basins rocking full of briny sea, the damp seeping into my very soul.

＊   ＊   ＊

of course as a prospective cadet i am asket questions.

for example: "have i filled in the correct application form?"

i nod.

the members of the panel look at me curiously.

not one of those gentleman can belive that i have actually dressed myself in a detachable startch't collar, mearly to bow my head in their shabby chappel and thus be knighted as an apprentice stonemason.

"are you awhere that you are applying for the postion of apprentice stonemason?"

again i nod in the afirmitive.

"why, there hasn't been an apprentice stone mason in the yard for, what? . . . 30 years?" musess the ginger comb-over.

"not in my life time" agrees dandruff collar.

"gentlemen, gentlemen!" interupts the one in the middle, raising his old claw: someone off stage tugs on a bit of string and up it goes like a wooden spatchular. and then he moves his lips as well, like a ventriliquists dummy. you can even see the little cut marks down the sides of his mouth, and inside, a little row of real bone teeth.

they huddle and have another conflab. fresh matches are struck and extra plumes of smoke arranged over their shiny bonces. small shafts of lite aluminate the clouds at different levels.

whole vistas and hevenly relmes are
hinted at in those sulferious swirrls.

i sit thru the debate looking from
one indistinckt face to the other.

it seams that they have forgotten
all about me, that i have become
invisible, or at least shrouded in
tobacco smoke.

theres lots of 'betwixed and
between' about this mythological
stonemason of theirs. everything is
speculative. one would susspeck't that
skollars of homers poem would be more
sure of the sepperation between fact and
myth.

i watch them disappearing and
reappearing thru the fog.

back and forth range the arguments.
it is as if the whole of life is just
some fancy smoke screen puffed out of the
mouth of god, purely to confound a young
fellow. so it is, sat there trying to
draw sence out of madness.

after much discussion it is
assatained that there mite actually
be a stonemason still practicing in
the dockyard. but no one knows fore
defineite if he is alive or dead. one of
the gentleman of the panel, old snow-
flakes, is convinced that this so-called
stonemason is only a rumour, or quasi
legend. and it isn't until a clark is
sent to the file room and re-appears

with some ancient enrolment ledger that
it is established that a certain bill
cubitt was indeed indentured as a master
stonemason in the summer of 1927. on
august the 6ᵗʰ, to be precise.

"are you absolutely sure you filled
in the correct application form?" asks
comb-over, "wouldn't you preffer to be a
'bricky'?"

i look to him wide eyed. "no, sir"
i answer, "stonemasonry is the life for
me."

he checks my face, cearfully. i
pinch a smile and he looks back down at
the leather bound ledger. the riting in
there is really quite intricate. copper
plate, all hand done with a quill.

why they cant belive in my honest
desire to toughen up my hands with hard
graft, i dont know.

this is what its like to be
interviewed by puppets in a smoke screen.
if you took a hammer to the window and
let some fresh air in here they mite just
all blow away like scotch mist.

by now it must be clear that i never
wanted to come to this interview in the
1ˢᵗ place.

at 9.30, i walked passed the ques
for apprentice electrision, bricky,
boiler maker, etc, etc, came in thru
those big polished doors, walk't up past

the stairway, along the echoing corridor
and sat in their blasted waighting
room alone. there i had to sit rubbing
my fingers together listening to the
muttering and hacking coughs coming from
these intombed fossels. then my name was
called and i was ushered in: the only
applicant.

if i was a bird sat in a tree
outside that window, peeping in at this
strange seen: 3 old men, all sparking up
fresh fags, billowing smoke left right
and center, scratching their hairy lug-
holes with their biros, and riting little
pertinent obsivations down on sheeves of
ivory coloured valour, well, i'd thank
my luckey stars for the gift of flight,
feathers and tall trees.

and all the while the hopefull
cadet, in this case myself, looks out of
the window for a sign of his frends.

is it rite, one wonders, to have
strange men scrutinize you and ask you
a lot of silly questions that you cant
truthfully answer without impeaching
yourself?

notice that this cadet is a mear
youth, wearing a short back and sides,
a starched collar and studs, cufflinks
and his fathers blazer from the back end
of the 1940's. realy we have to wonder
in what age our tale is taking place.
also his fathers raf trousers, from his
national servis days, are swinging from

an ancient pair of braces.

what a spectical!

am i animating my fathers corpse?

not that my father is dead of
course, but in many ways he is.

poeticly he is dead. but also his
very much alive, mainly in my mothers
fears.

of course im over dressed for
my interview, sat like a ghost from
the past. im a throw back, a living
anachronisim. a memory. very much dressed
as these old gentlemen themselves, in
fact.

if not a bird at the window, then
imagin being an ant scurrying about, then
nestling in a crack in the pavement,
avoiding hard boots and all sorts of
blows from above.

are not ants, by their very nature,
more suited to live in mounds of twigs
and dirt in woodland clearings, where
the air is a little fresher and tainted
only with the sent of pine rather than
the stench of petrol and diesel? but also
the hard beak of a jay is a terryfing
spectical.

to the unprobing mind it would
appear that animels have an easy life.
and indeed they do: even if hunted
they remain somehow 'carefree'. this is

presisly becouse they are un awaear that
they have a life of hardship. felling
trapped by suffering is the hefty lump,
not the suffering.

or imagin being a squirrel in a
tree. a red squirrel with black ear tufts
and a nice thrusting tail and a warm nest
to curl up in. you hear the creaking of
the tree as you sleep. and outside the
great pine forest is alive with your
cousins - all the animels you can fancy.
even a jay sat on a twig outside your
front door when you awake in the morning
is not a threat, and you know how to
collect nuts even if you cant be bothered
to count them, and you dont have to go
to skool and have your squirrel nature
corrupted by the lazyness of uniformity.

and that, gentlemen, is my point:
is it really so bad to lack an education?
whats really hard is to be made to attend
skool just for the hell of it, becouse
no one in our skool of over 700 pupels
was on the resiving end of one. we were
designated dockyard fodder on the day
our 11 year old eyes, heads, hands and
feet passed under that iron gateway which
read:

freddom thru education.

of course it didn't.

over the way was the girls skool:
another 700 no-hopers waiting to drop
their knickers, get knockt-up and hate
us for it into the bargain. isnt that a

little crude and inelagant of me? yes,
but im aluding to something - pointing
with a stinking finger towards . . . i
dont know, something proberbly base and
not worth mentioning.

but what about the free education
of god and the universe? - the sort of
knowledge you dont have to subdue your
hart for because it just rots down with
the humus and you eat it up with the
seeds and nuts and it invigorates your
sap without you even noticing.

isnt that worth something?

after all, a squirrel knows how to
be a squirrel and a nut knows how to be
a nut, and neither one of them feels any
the less, or cheated by god, or nature,
for it.

does the nut hate the squirrel for
eating it? of course not. and thats how
it is for a skool boy: he smiles as his
eaten. but of course there are hidden
resentments.

a secondary modern skool is a place
where children are ground down into
dust then simply blown away. naturally
the same can be said of all skools, but
whereas a grammer skool blows the dust
into the doorways of a cosy university,
art skool or comely high street bank, we
secondary skool kids get blown in thru
the dockyard gates by a cold gust.

its our birthrite, handed down

thru the generations like a curse, and
you may as well hate newts for having the
audasity of giving birth to tadpoles that
inturn mutated into our grandparents, for
all the good it will do you to fight it.

scoopt from a nice bed of leafs,
then held merclissly in clawed fists, the
hapless nut looks up into the furry face
of its attacker, whos cruel lips curl
back revealing great buck teeth, which
smash down like mighty claw hammers. in
effect, beheading the defencless nut.

just so, universal love was not as
glowing and apperent upon the fizogs of
our irritable teachers as jesus might
have proscribed. but was it their job
alone to love us, is not love after all a
dialogue with the self?

maybe if we, as cained and stropped
children, had loved and forgiven our
toementors - and turned the other
cheek, as it were - then love could have
blossomed within our skool teachers
harts and the wonders of learning been
effortlessly transmuted into our rude and
furtive minds.

so far no such experiments have been
undertaken.

          ❋   ❋   ❋

in my 5th and final year at skool 7veral
letters were sent to my parents stating
that i was a hopeless case and beyond
redeption. even my estranged father put
in an apperence at the skool and agreed
with their prognosses.

never-the-less, my dust had to be
swept someplace.

for this purpose me, and my usless
classmates, were sent along to see the
carrers officer, whos job it was to find
us 'positions' in the outside world.

our form teacher, mrs cooper,
calls the class register. she stands
out front dressed in her skin tight
riding breaches. nothing left to the
imagination. i look out the window at the
gale blowing amongst the trees and answer
my name resignedly. theres an old egg
carton cartwheeling along the ground. it
goes rite across the field at full tilt
then pinned against the skool fence.

a moniter hands round slips of pink
gerstetner paper. i glance down. there is
my name and a time ritten there in red
biro on a dotted line.

"now you all have your piece of
paper. at the apointed time you are to
proceed, without talking or running in
the corridoor, to the sience room, which
has been re-designated the carreers
office. there you will knock quitly and
awaite the instruction to enter."

i look at her and curl the pink
sugery paper in my hand. you can see
every detail of her virgina.

*   *   *

we sit thru maths and re, then its break.
even though the gale is going full pelt
the teachers still force us out onto the
cold tarmac.

youed think that when its icy cold
youed at least be allowed to stay in
class, but you most certainly are not.
even during lessons your not allowed to
wear your outdoor coat, nor warm your
arse on the raditors. and chances are the
radiators arnt really cranked up anyways,
and we sit at our desks shivering. then
the bell goes and they chuck us outside
again.

we hunch our shoulders and turn our
back to the wind, then it starts hailing
as well. our faces are properly stinging
from the icy stones.

most of us crowd in under the porch,
pushing up against the doors, but the
barstard prefects just laugh at us from
the other side of the reinforced glass
and keep us out rite up until the end of
break bell goes.

by afternoon break everyone in

my class has already seen the carreers
officer. i look at the clock on the wall
and check the time: 5 past 3, and a
small, apologetic looking figure crosses
the skool playground, leaning into the
hurrican. i put my hand up and head off
to my appointment.

for all her child-like qualitys
i have to tell you that my mother has
painted quite a dark and unplesent
picture of my life and future. "its the
survial of the fittest!" she intones,
banging her fist on the table.

since i was 7 she's also been
telling me that she'd rob a bank if she
could get away with it. "you have to plan
the perfict crime." she adds.

yes, my family are all criminals of
one stripe or another.

also, she lives in the honest belief
of our imminent destruction.

she comes in thru the main entrance
patting down her dishevelled hair. rite
from the get go it is obvious that she's
done herself up espesherly for the
occasion: for one, nanna lewis's lank fur
coat is draped over her shoulders, and
for 2, she has smeered on that orange
coloured lipstick that smells of sick and
violets.

but despite her best efforts my
mothers eyes are sad and worried looking,
and her inbread timidness, expressed by

the way that her hand clutches at her
throat, reveal that she is a victim of
life, and she would like me to join her.

yes, she is togged-up to make a
grand impression.

instead of looking squarly into the
eyes of the world and saying 'i am here
to do my best by my son, and i expect
nothing less from you weak charletons',
my mothers posture says 'excuse me, im
sorry for waisting your time and hope
that my sons existance is not too much of
an inconvenience to you.' and then she
lowers her mouth and murmers sorry into
the collar of her mothers lank fur coat.

how sad it all makes a son feel
to know that his brow-beaten mother is
behind him, willing him on, as it were
into success and failure.

if only she could have stayed at
home and left me to my fate, because she
certainly isnt interested in fighting my
corner.

enough is enough. rather than
feeling embariced i should of course be
greatfull. after all not all mothers
obseve this part of their parental duty.
in point of fact i am the only boy in the
entire skool to have his mummy come and
hold his hand for him.

also, according to my mother, my
father is on holliday in maritious with
his mistress. "his with her now! spending

our money! his lordship swans off to
sun himself whilest im left stuck here
bringing up his bluddy kids!"

its all perfectly true.

i have to listen to her hissing
whisper as we cross the quadrangle.

a class of kids gawp out the window
at us and i lower my head to make myself
smaller but to my shame i am already 6
inches taller than my poor mother.

we walk down the corridor to the
sience room.

all in all i find my mothers
presence unessissary and humiliating.

when we arrive theres a little
ginger kid sat outside. his name is
melcom cowthorpe. i nod to him. i used
to go to infantes skool with cowthorpe
in the olden days. we compare pices of
paper. my slip has got an earlier time on
than his so i get to go in 1st.

my mother interupts and says that i
should let cowthorpe go in 1st, as he was
here before us. i explain to her that we
have our appointment times ritten down
and show her my slip of paper. she looks
at it then repeats that cowthorpe was
here 1st. i get melcom to show my mother
his slip of paper, which is timed 15
minits after mine, in case she is too
stupid to understand.

"its alrite," say's melcom, "gustov
is before me."

"yes, but you were here 1ˢᵗ" repeats
my mother.

"melcom was here befor us, but its
not his turn." i explain.

my mother goes very tight lipped. "im
sorry i spoke!"

"no, it really is gustovs turn
next," repeats the ginger nut.

"i may as well not say anything,"
sulks my mother.

i look at her hurt childs face, turn
and knock on the door. a muffeld voice
says 'enter'.

sat there behind the teachers desk
is a rotund little fellow with greeced
dark hair and a large, indolent mouth.
by those blubbery lips we boys are to be
blown hither and thither.

rite off my mother starts in
apologising for our coming in before the
other boy. this completely confuses the
carreers officer, who stands, goes to the
door and asks to see cowthorpe's slip of
pink sugar paper. he pushes a thick pair
of glasses on his nose and stands their
compairing them.

"but it says gustov claudius, 3.15
and you are?"

"gustov claudius," i reply.

"and the time is?"

"3.15, sir."

"well get in there boy, and stop
messing around!" and he raises his hand
as if to clump me one, and my mother
jerks her head in agreement.

i cant help but feel that the main
reason for my mother acompaning me is to
make sure that i get into trouble, and
to apologise to the carreers officer for
waisting his time and efforts.

"sit down, for hevens sakes." and
he pulls another chair out for my mother.
"im mister beuys."

"thank you, for yor time," says my
mother.

"thats quite allrite, mrs . .
. claudius." and he dose a big fake
smile, parks himself behind the desk and
scrutinises me with a frown.

"your name and time were ritten on
your slip?"

"yes i know. it was a
misunderstanding."

"there is no misunderstanding. if
you cant be punctual in skool how do you
expect to function in the outside world?
employers wont tolerate lateness or
absenteisim."

mister beuys studies my slip of
paper again and compairs it to a list on
his desk.

"so you are . . . gustov?" and he
looks sharply at me.

"yes, im still him."

beuys looks at me coldly "it says
here that your appointment is at 3.15 and
its now . . ." and mister boyce flicks
his rist out and checks his watch, "3.20,
by my watch. i think we'll have to buy
him a watch, mrs claudius."

and my mother smiles at his great
joke.

"i dont want to butt in," explains
my mother, "not if the other boy is
before us. we can go and waight outside
if its a problem," and she goes to get
up.

"no, please, its your turn. please
sit down, we'er running late already."

my mother concedes the point and
stays seated. basicly she is seeking
redemption - on my beharf - for my diming
the lites of the entire planet.

beuys turns to me again. "you need
to listen to your mother, lad, and waight
your turn. now, what are you looking for.
what area of employment interests you?"

"art college."

"further education? i see. well you haven't really got the qualifications for that, have you, my lad?"

he chuckles and looks to my mother for a reaction. seeing her fearfull eyes he shakes his head and laughs a bit louder. "what an idear!"

my mother nods in worried agreement.

"never-the-less, i'd still like to go to art college." i say levely.

"to study what, tecknical drawing?"

"no, painting."

"painting! what, pictures?" and beuys really dose pull a ridiclious face.

then, mirracliousely my mother raises her worried face and whispers, "he wants to be an artist."

"an artist?"

"a painter," she replys.

"no, come on. i dont think your going to make a living doing doodles, lad. of course you can do your art in your spair time, but im talking about actual werk. your not in kinda garden now."

"his elder brother paints," says my mother, determinedly. "he is studdying at art skool."

"really? at art college?"

"yes," she whispers.

the careers officer nods and scratches his cheek.

"and what skool did . . . gustovs elder brother attend? obviously not w - secondary skool."

"oh no, he went to g - grammer."

beuys puts his fingers together, leans back in his chair and gives a sacrin smile.

"well there you are, that explains it. that explains everything."

"how do you mean?" i put in.

"your elder brother obvioulsy achived exam results."

"yes." says my mother.

"o-levels?"

"yes, 9."

"9!" the carreers officer nods approvingly. "and a-levels?"

"3."

"3? excilent!" beuys turns to me again, "9 o-levels, and 3 a-levels, gustov. and how many o-levels are you taking?" he asks with a very patronising air.

"one."

"one!" and he smiles to my mother.

"he does like his drawing," my
mother murmers.

out of respect for my mother beuys
pretends to be listening to what she has
to say, before dismissing her with a wave
of his fingers.

"thats all very interesting,
mrs claudius, but im afraid its
qualifications, qualifications and
qualifications these days. thats all they
are interested in. you cant get into
further education without them. plain and
simple, done and dusted! those, im afraid
are the cold facts."

beuys pulls a sheet of paper from a
blue card folder and quickly runs over it
with the tip of his biro.

"looking at gustov's end of term
report his teachers are uneqivacable that
he stands absolutely no hope of achiving
any meaningfull exam results. let alone
those nessisary, and required, to gain
him entrance into an art skool."

mister beuys looks up trumphantly
at my mother, then allows his eyes to
travel sidways and cock their lids at me.

it is possible to detect a superiour
smerk playing round his fat lips.

"i told you," my mother whispers at

me. then turning to the carreers officer.
"i told him that he had to learn to read
and rite, but he wouldnt listen. he
thinks he knows it all. you cant tell him
any thing!"

"im afraid your mother is rite
again, lad. exam results! thats what an
employer, or university . . . or art
skool, wants to see."

theres a silence as my mother goes
into her handbag for her small flowery
handkerchief. i feel the inside of my
teeth with my tounge.

the carreers officer flings his rist
out again and checks his watch. "perhaps
your son should set his sites a little
lower, mrs claudius. the dockyard, for
instance."

"yes," my mother says, brightening
up considerably. "my father, his
grandfather, was in the dockyard. its
good in there. its good." and her cheecks
flush with excitement.

"just what i always say, mrs
claudius." and beuys licks his
forefinger, and shuffles about in his
card index. "i . . . mite . . . just . .
. have . . . something . . . yes, heres
what i was looking for!" and he plucks
out the only card in there which actually
seams to have anything ritten on it.

"the yard has some alluring
prospects for a young person 1st stepping

onto the carreer ladder. there are some
very interesting openings for labouring
you know."

   "are there any apprentisships?"
whispers my mother.

   beuys looks at her doubtfully.
"yes . . . but they also require
qualifications. wouldnt labouring be a
bit more . . . "

   "what appentisships are there? i
saw some in the newspaper," interupts my
mother.

   beuys sighs and looks down at the
list. "well, it says here, boiler maker,
bricklaying, caulker, electrician,
fitter, roapmaker, stonemason, sale
maker, etc, etc . . ."

   i stand up and lean over the desk.
mister beuys attempts to shield the card
from my view.

   "what is that ritten at the bottom?"

   "nothing of interest." and he holds
the card to his chest.

   "did you say stonemason?"

   beuys checks the card, still
shelding it from my view. "maybe. yes, in
fact it is. as it happens."

   beuys peers again at the card and
this time lifts his glasses. "you know,
ive never seen that before. do you

suppose theres really such a job? ile
have to check. it could be a clerical
error."

"i would like to aply to be a
stonemasons apprentice in the dockyard."
i say it very firmly.

"you'ed still need the required
qualifications. or at least to pass the
entrance exam. are you sure you wouldnt
be interested in labouring - people will
always need laboures." and beuys looks
expectantly at my mother, who nods on
que.

i stair at her.

"thou of course you cant tell him
anything," she pleads to beuys, "his
like his sodding, bleeding father!"

that, as they say, is the bottom
line.

*   *   *

skooling the debris of albion

no, i will not be allowed to apply to
art skool and i have no one to blame but
myself.

there is an endless list of my

deficentsys.

top most, i was not partial to
getting up in the mornings. this was
largly due to lack of sleep brought about
by fear of vampires, which in turn was
brought about by being submerged into the
world of sex by a male adult when i was
9, and the subsquent bed wetting.

of course, not every child thus
indoctrinated loses the ability to add
up, or read and rite.

and it is true that i liked to
distract the direction of lessons by the
insection of what mister gorf termed 'red
herrings'.

also, i was bullied and had to avoid
ambushes. this can make a fellow doubly
late. you see, all my skool days i was
always checking for escape routes.

is that melodramatic?

so what if it is. in the playground
the weight of a fist is quite perswasive.
in the classroom a wooden board rubber
flung at your head by a teacher who hates
children leaves its own indentations.

in fairness, it must be said that
our teachers were mearly trying - in the
wurst of circumstances - to smash any
idotic notions of fairness from our heads
and get us ready for the chop.

with this in mind we were assured

that thou our skool boy lifes mite seam
to be missrable, inaine, unfair and
utterly pointless, our current experence
was nothing compaired to the excilent
drubbing that was going to smack us
in the face on the other side of the
skoolyard gate.

was this a warning born of genuine
teacherly concern?

from reading these last few lines
some will affirm that i have again
allowed sarcasim to colour the point of
my pencil.

all i am trying to say is this:
it would have been plesent to have
been loved and valued as children, and
encouraged to think and feel and laugh
and enjoy life.

but thats costly stuff. our teachers
would never allow it. why, it mite lead
to certain expressions and oppinons.
and as my mother has oft pointed out
'oppinions only lead to conflickt!'

of course, my mother has never
expressed such a terse sentiment in her
life, but she did repeatedly knock it
into my head that i was in for a rude
awakening, and that it would be best for
me to knuckle down and stop antagonising
people.

but despite being instructed to
underestimate my potentcial and apologise
for breathing i have still had the nurve

to dissobay my mother, and so conflict
has thrown its generious arms about me.

does that make me unique and
special?

when i tell you that my mother
was sobbing because our father left
home i, her little boy, had to gingerly
put my arm round her and tell her that
everything would be alrite.

again im casting stones. it is
preposterious to surgest that my mother
never loved me or that our teachers were
all violent werewolfs.

but, if ever there were to be a
judical review into the skooling of
'the debris of albion' the prosicutor
would not be able acuse our teachers of
laxity when it came to the 'laying on of
the rod'. nor were blushes spaired when
violent predictions were employed as
a means of suppressing any imaginative
potentaial peeping from the resesses of
our thick sculls.

and my mother? it will be said that
she was too bissy planning her nurvous
breakdown to have time to notice her
youngest son being sexually abused.

        *   *   *

so now i fix on my fathers starched

collar, knot my tie and pull on a pair of
his national servis trousers. next i don
his old skool blazer and set off for my
interview.

and all the while my mother fuss's
about me, hovering like some infernal
blow fly.

certainly, by the way these puppet
heads are looking me up and down it is
possible to decern their confusion,
and imagin them asking themselves -
'stonemasons apprentice? isnt this young
man not too well dressed and worldly
intelligent for such a lowly postion?'

and so the world is fooled.

into the yard

a section of putty had been freshly
dug out of the metal window frame and a
dead wasp lay curled there. in the last
throws of death it had been stabbing
itself with its own sting.

a skool boy yawns and stares out
of the rain flect window at some distent
trees waving their stick fingers in the
wind and drizzle.

how will life be one wonders, i mean
when it really gets going? can it really
be that 1 in 3 of us is for the nut house
like that visiting phycatrist said in the
libary. and mister b. smith stood there
in front of the entire class and told him
that i was a prime candadete.

despite everything i am still
somewhat unafraid of the world and the
tribulations of 'the werking life' as it
is so coyly termed. it is as if all the
threats and unhappyness promised us is
somehow destined for others but not for
me.

if the only option open to us
retards is the dockyard then so be it, i
will bite down on their magotty apple and
chew thortfully, before spitting it in
the gutter.

and what if i am punished and
bullied in werk as i have been in skool?
why, i will riggle and prance, and like
a boxing kangeroo, outshine my werk mates
with nimble faints, surprising agilitys,
and thus sidestep my oppressors to be
recognised as unique and special.

it is possible for me to predict
all of this becouse somehow the gods
will look kindly upon me, and so i will
be pluckt from the fiary flames of hell,
bearly singed.

is it possible to be special? no not
really.

even tho in many ways i have been
unspeakably cruel. for instance, the
spirits of wasps and ants will be after
me in particular. but still, its not too
late to make amends, and perhaps lay out
some tasty suger for them to suck upon in
recompence.

*   *   *

monday morning i get up at 6.

my mother makes me my cheese
sandwiches and a flask of tea, and i
head off down to the bus stop. i have
to change buses at the town center. my
connection isnt in yet so i look into the
window of the tabaconist then cross m -

road.

the town hall rises up like a
soft mushroom, or chalk cliff, or stone
cloud - depending on your sencibillitys
- with a clock way up on top, balanced
there next to the sky. somewhere, beyond
guilded doorways, wood paneled chambers
and dark vestabules, lies the mayor, sat
there wearing an ermin muff, his big
gold chain and puffing away on a big fat
cigar, i imagin.

i peer in thru the gloom of the
entrance, say what you like, for all his
finery hes still living in a hermits
cave!

how shall i live?

how shall i become someone?

will anyone follow me?

will i be forever alone?

a man, for instance, isnt the
easyist thing to be.

will i make cave paintings?

will i become a master mason?

just then the dockyard bus passes.
i look and check that the town hall clock
is correct. there is no more time for
questions and debate. i turn on my heel
and engage my trim calfs, heading off up
dock road looking over my shoulder for a
taxi.

you see, to be late could get you
in peoples bad books. my mother has
installed that much in me.

not that im at all worried. but late
on your 1st day? that wouldn't do at all.
maybe start slacking after you've got
your feet under the table - yes, thats
the time to relax, but now is the time to
show willing.

i stay close to the road, trotting
along, one foot tripping in the gutter,
my neck twisted over my shoulder.
theres nothing but bikes streaming past,
clogging up the whole street and not a
cabbie in site. this really is getting to
be quite serious. my hart starts to throb
in my throat and i feel the desire to
start crying.

then a taxi finnaly apperes. it
comes out of the distence. i wave at him
like a scearcrow. he pulls into the layby
ahead.

i catch up gasping and peer in
thru the side window. the driver has a
crumpeled yellow face with a ciggeret in
it.

i decide it is best to ride in the
back and climb in.

"where to?" and the ciggeret wobbles
up and down as he speaks.

"the dockyard, please."

the cabbie studdiys me in his rear

view mirror.

"the dockyard?" he drawls.

"yes, please."

"its only up the bleeding road - you can walk it in 1/2 the time," he says contemptusly.

"its my 1st day, im late." i hold up my rist for him to see, thou im not actually wearing a watch.

he scowls at me, puffs out a great plume of blue smoke and jams the car into gear.

"its your bleeding money!" and without looking he pulls out into the stream of angry traffic, narrowly missing an old codger on a penny fathing.

"look where your going, you cows son! bikes, nothing but bleeding bikes!"

straight away he does some very intricate manover that manages to get us wedged behind a big green bus. we crawl along, the needle twitching on 5 miles an houre.

i look at the bus hungerely. shouldn't i ask the cabbie to pull over, so's i can just jump out and catch the bus instead? its doing the same speed as us and it would cost me a fraction of the price. i would like to speak up, but somehow im afraid to make the driver angry.

instead i content myself with
studdying the creases in the back of
his sunburnt neck. they show up whitish
against the yellow/brown of his tan.

maybe he'd like to shoot the breeze
about the weather, then perhaps he'll get
a bit friendlier and concidor letting
me out so's i can jump on the green bus
instead. i cough so as to attract his
attension, but he is intent on ignoring
me.

instead i studdy his drivers eyes,
which i can see moving in his rear view
mirror. are they the eyes of a man who
will happly pull over, let me jump out,
then wish me good luck on the 1st day
of my werking life and cry "hurry along
mind! dont worry about those few yards
we've travelled, have them on the house!
you hop on that bus, son. oh, and heres
50p to cover your bus fair"? it seams
not.

i start nibbling at my lips. we
really are going to be terrificly late.
even the bikes are overtaking us.

its as if the driver has jamed his
stupid car, and inadiquet brain, into
reverse.

i look out at all the grim faces
peddling past. each old prune is suckt
quite dry, and their white knuckels
grip onto their rusty handle bars as if
hanging onto the last thread of life.

you have to smile when you see their
bandy legs going 19 to the dozen.

others mite look upon this very
same seen and declair that each and
every werker appears as if inbewed with
an inner quiet and dignity, but anyone
who really used their eyes would see
their cheeks are puffing out like old
paper bags, and each turn of the peddles
brings them closer to ingraving their own
headstone.

if you think about it, compaired to
all those bikes swarming along heading
for the dockyard, its as if im the only
prince on the highways.

"everyone takes a bleeding cab now
days!" mutters the cabbie. i look at
his sticky out ears. he is obviously
angry that im not puffing along outside
suffering on a push bike with them.

"it must be good for you, thou."
i say hopfully, "getting extra fairs, i
mean."

the cabbie sneers, stubs out his fag
in the over flowing ashe tray and lites
another.

"i drove a bunch of those bleeding
borstal boys up the bleeding prision last
week. a cab? they should make em bleeding
walk!"

"on their bare feet," i add.

he looks at me in his rear view
mirror and wrinkels his brows.

"so that there feet bleed," i
explain.

the cabbie trys to think about my
prepossel, scowls and relites his fag,
that has somehow gone out.

"its the principle of the f-ing
matter. they'er criminals. thats tax
payers money. in bleeding handcuffs they
were!"

i notice a little union jack stuck
on his dash board, and theres a paper
air freshner in the shape of a fur tree
dangling from his mirror, battling
to bring the fragrent scents of a
scandanavian forrest to the interriour of
what is in effect a giant ash-tray.

we stop start all the way up dock
road, waighting for the bus as it crams
on another 6 passangers.

outside the window i see a pidgion
lurking by a puddle. it gets splashed
by a passing bike wheel and with a
sudden dash gallops over the paving
slabs and overtakes us on foot. i stair
unbelievingly, but it really is true: a
pidgion is racing us to the dockyard gate
on foot. one of those feet is gnarled
and deformed, and it is already 2 cars
lengths ahead of us.

the bus pulls away in slow motion

and the cabbie casually lets about 30
bikes pile in between us, so we miss any
chance of overtaking this club-footed
racing pidgion.

absolutely increadible.

eventualy we pull up outside the
main gate. theres no sign of the pidgion,
and scearsly room to open the door
amongst the great gaggle of black push
bikes that pours past us.

"75p!"

and the driver lites up yet another
ciggeret.

i rummidge around in my pockets.
really, that should be about 50p at most.
i have to give him all my spair coppers.
i hand it over in a pile of lose change.
he looks at the pennys like as if they
was dirt.

"hardly worth my bleeding time! you
could of walkt it. getting a cab? you got
bleeding legs, intcha?"

i try to smile at him but its
pointless.

"you could ask the prison officer to
hancuff them to the bumper."

"do what?"

"the borstal boys. they could chain
them up in a line and make then pull the
taxi."

he curles his lip and taps his
forehead. "your fucking doolally, son,
fucking doolally!" and he pulls out,
rite infront of another stream of bikes,
who have to jam their breaks on to avoid
going arse over tit.

      *   *   *

i pick my way thru the heaving throng.
the airs cold at that time in the morning
- straight off the river like that. in
the olden days id of still been tuckt
up in my nice warm bed. is this what
all those grown-ups ment when they told
me that i was in for a rude awakening?
really? i chuckle to myself at the idocy
of them all, a little bit of cold air
isn't going to kill me.

i pass in under that gateway. thats
some crest they've got hanging up there:
20 ft across and all painted up in gold
leaf: a lion and a unicorn prancing about
like as if they've sprung from some kind
of vivid fairy tale. your'll know that
gate it is if you see it, its the only
one of its's kind. and a flag pole on
top, flapping the queens blanket: a site
to make the ordinary man touch his hart
and salute lord nelson.

whole groups of werkers race up
behind me. old men with ears and noses
enlarged by life - some still sporting

mons quiffs - effortlesssly hop off their
bikes and wheel them in thru the arch,
eyes cast down. they show their passes,
hacking up green stuff and gobbing it in
the gutters. i look down at the colours:
a whole row of gleaming dockyard oysters
with yellow eyes.

im not sure where to go so i join
the end of a que and copy the ones
infront of me. there're about 20 of them,
all in cloth caps and bicycle clips.
of course 7veral rough sorts push in
owing to my timidity but i am inexrably
moving towards that little keosk with the
window.

when its my turn, i take my pass
from inside my overalls - they'er quite
old style, last worn by a macanic werking
on a spitfire, i should imagine - and
present it to the little hitler sat there
behind his sliding window. he has his
medel ribons neatly sewn on and a shinny
peeked hat, yet for all his officiousness
he dosnt even bother looking at my
brand new government pass - yes, i have
signed the offical secreats act - but
heven knows why i even bothered as he
just waves me thru without a cear in the
world.

security certanly is lax, i could be
anyone.

i look around for someone to
turn to, but know one is the least bit
interested and the tide just shoves me

on thru. you come out from under that
gateway and rite away theres an ancient
ships figure head looming at you with a
great big oaken kisser, painted up kind
of gaurdy, like a prostitute.

actually, theres ships figure heads
scattered here abouts and everywhere.
you see, the idiots smashed up the ships
and only kept the mugs and you see them
mooching around this little green like as
if they'er the cast of some horror show
been invited to the admrils garden party.
grotesque but quite butifull really.

i pick my way down the cobbeled
streets. you have to watch your ankels
treading over those babys heads and im
only wearing bumper boots.

theres a train track at the bottom
and the admrals gaff, all grand with
its flags and pennents flapping. theres
even a little wooden awning to stop him
getting his cocket hat wet when he gets
in and out of his staff car.

people are streaming everywhere,
disappearing into dark doorways and
manholes.

i peer about looking for a sign
post, but there isn't one.

i ask a matlow the way to the psa
office, where im supposed to report, but
he dosnt answer. actually, his holding
a rifel and hisses at me to piss off.
whilest im waighting for a civel reply

another matlow marches up and halts rite
in front of me. this one's wearing a full
beared and 3 stripes on his arm.

"cant you see he's on guard. what do
you want?"

i explain to him that im a new
apprentice and im looking for the psa
office.

"office! you mean cabin, your not
on land now, jimmy green. besides, your
miles away."

"really?"

"you come in thru the rong gate,
forstarters. this is the main gate, you
want the c - gate."

"i thort they were the same thing."

"you can think what you like, boy,
it dont make it so, dose it!"

i look at him. "thats quite true,
but all the same are you sure?" i ask.

the matlow gives a grunt, spits on
the ground and walks away, his trousers
flapping like a pair of black tents.

i look at the other matlow, still
stood there not blinking an eye lid.

ridiculious!

seriously, despite my cearfree
aproach im still a little afraid of being

late, of being reprimanded and being cast
as 'the rong sort' from the outset.

i trot along at quite a gallop, my
scran bag - contaning a red cross 1st aid
tin filled with cheese sandwidges rapped
in greece-proof paper and a tarten flask
of tea - banging away on my shoulders.

allthough extra worrid, i even
have a slight sweat on, in many ways i
couldn't cear less if im late for there
stupid job. so what if i get the sack
on the spot? arnt there plenty of other
openings in the world for a keen young
artist? besides, its hardly my fault
that they have 3 different entrances to
their ridiclious dockyard, one of them
apparently being in a different town!

i see plently of battle ships, all
painted up in crab fat and mored to the
quay-side. the waters quite black in the
basins, with plenty of oil slicks.

now and then theres a glimps of open
water: a smoky old hulk, mored to a bouy
since nelsons time, is rotting away out
in midstream - a ghost ship in the fog.

i pass under rows of iron gray
crains on rail tracks - none of them
werking yet as everyone's gone to ground
to scoff their breakfasts.

after another mile or so i spot a
green sign with psa works dept, stenciled
on it in white lettering. thats where im
ment to be. i put on an extra lick and

hurry over.

theres a whole gang of brickys apprentices hanging about outside, all swearing smoking and kicking at each other. 2 or 3 of the older ones stand to one side and practicie spitting, eaffecting an air of serfistication and studied indifference.

i slow down as i come up to them and try to be invisible. i stair down at the ground most diligently but one of them, with ferocious acni, shoves his mate into me and he in turn knocks me aside.

"pete, what are you doing - you knockt over the little gentleman." says acni face, the one who shoved him into me in the 1st place.

"sorry about him, mate!" and he leers agresivly in my face.

all in all its a fantasticly funny joke.

i get my mitt on the door handle quick as you like, incase they've got flick knives.

"new apprentice?" asks acni chops. i notice that he has a da and is wearing an earing. no one wears ear rings except teddy boys.

i nod without looking him in the eye.

"bricky?" he barks.

"no, stonemason," i reply weakly,
and have to cough.

"stonemason? what the fucks a
stonemason?"

i open the door and push in, "ive
got to report to the 'cabin'. im late.
they sent me to the rong gate."

i let the door swing too behind me.

theres a fellow sat in there behind
an ancient wooden riting desk leafing
thru a vast open ledger. i walk over and
stand to attention in front of him. he
has very red ears and looks for all the
world like our old geography teacher,
mister gorf. only with shorter hair, a
bigger nose, and he has a shaving rash on
his adams apple where as mister gorf wore
a mustashe.

he looks up at me with an air of
tired irritation.

"whats all that noise about out
there?"

"just some apprentices larking
about."

"well go out there and tell them to
shut up!"

i look at this new mister gorf.
"me?"

"well im not talking to the wall, am i!"

i go pop my head back round the door.

"excuse me!"

7veral of them have a small apprentice held upside down by his legs and acni chops with the earing is pulling his trousers off.

"oi, you lot!!" i call out, only they'er not really listening. i shout louder, then louder still. finnaly, the one with an earring turns and fixes me with his 2 see-thru blue eyes, which god has placed a bit to close to the centre of his face. i try to smile in a friendly way. "excuse me, but the fellow in here ask't if you would mind keeping the noise down. he cant here himself bleeding think!"

i just get the door closed behind me before im collared and rughed up.

i go back over to the new mister gorfs desk.

rite away a group of faces press up against the window. the one with the ear ring is pointing at me and holding up his ginger coloured fist.

mister gorf jumps out of his chair, comes round his desk and marches out side. i stand by the door and listen

cearfully. you can here gorf barking at
them, then it all goes very quite and
then gorf comes back in dusting his hands
then straightning his tie.

he sits back back down and carrys on
leafing thru the pages of his ledger as
if he is quite alone in the universe and
that i never came and stood obedeantly
before his oaken desk.

i look down on him, examining the
crown of his head at the starting of a
bald patch but he still refuses to look
up and akknowlege me.

theres a clock on the wall and i
decide to watch the second hand of that
instead. it does 2 full circits, which is
120 seconds and still he's got his nose
jammed in that infernal ledger of his.

i decide to tell him my name anyway.
i cough and anonce myself and my mission.

this new mister gorf looks up
and blinks. it really is as if he is
genuinely supprized to see me.

despite my mothers prenouncments of
doom, here i am, bang on time, stood to
attention and ready to take my place in
the ranks of good honest werking men.

"i beg your pardon, who did you say
you were?"

i repeat my story: that im a new
apprentice. he nods slowly, thinking to

himself and flicks distractedly thru the
pages of his ledger.

"stonemasons apprentice. " i add.

"stonemason?" and he looks up again,
shocked. are you sure? we dont get many
of those. none really. not since . . .
well the war, i would imagine. "

he takes a ruler from the desk
draw, finds my name in the ledger and
underlines it with a pencil. he motions
towards some ancient looking chairs over
by the window and tells me to go and sit
down. the chairs have horse hair sticking
out in tufts and their collapsed seats
been nailed over with wooden planks.

"well sit down if your going to!"

i smile, the chairs look quite hard
and uncomfortable.

this new mister gorf already has his
head down again and is bisserly ritting
away at some tremendously important
treatese.

for some reason he wants me to
get out of his lite and go sit way over
here. most likly so's he can pratice his
wonderful penmanship. the chairs are not
the most luxsorius chaislounge ever seen.
i come and stand in front of his desk
once again and clear my throat. this time
he really gives me the eyeball.

i decide to explain to him that

the reason i mite be a little late is
not because ive slept in or anything
like that, but primerally becouse i was
dropped off at the rong gate by a very
slow, over charging taxi driver.

"thats how im late. if id of just
got the bus, or even walk't . . . plus
the gate man scearsly lookt at my pass."

"really" he says with exaggerated
interest before putting his nose back
into his ledger.

"yes, he just let me walk straight
in!"

the man who looks like mister gorf
drags his eye balls from the inky pages
and silently looks me up and down with
some dissdain

"of course, that didn't make me
late, in itself," i explain hurridly,
"in fact it sped things up a bit, if
anything. but still, its not exactly what
id call high security. i could have been
anyone. i could be a member of the ira
for all he knows."

this mister gorf itches the side
of his nose with the end of his pencil,
which has a small green rubber on it,
then drums his front teeth with his
short, bitten nails.

to tell the absolute truth he
dosnt look that much like mister gorf at
all. for starters his nose is way too

big, his hairs too long - plus its the
rong colour, and its texture is far too
course. plus the real mister gorf always
wore a tan cordroy jacket with leather
elbow patches, where as this imposter is
sat in a cheep looking pin-stipped suit.

"you say he didn't check your pass
propperly?" and this mister gorf rites
something down in the margin of his
ledger, next to my name. i try to look at
what he's ritten, but he puts his arm in
the way.

"no, he basicly ignored my pass,
and me."

"ignored you?" and this mister gorf
lets out a low whistle.

he seams a little more interested
in this part of my story so i give a run
down of the events and a full description
of the gate man so's that he can be
reprimanded, and if nessissary, sacked
for gross incomptence.

"so he's quite a slacker, this gate
man of yours."

"i dont want to get anyone into
trouble, or anything."

"of course you dont. did you take
his name, perchance?"

"no." i answer quite shocked. "i
didn't think of that.

"his number?"

"no," i mumble looking down at
my plimpsols. "i didn't think of that
either. but he did have little numbers on
his collar." i add, brightening up.

"and what was his number?"

"i cant remember. i forgot to rite
it down" i add appologetickly, "but there
was a 6 in it, and i think it mite have
been made of brass and ended in a 3, i
think."

"brass, really? and a number 3? my,
my, my." and mister gorfs twin brother
also rites this down in the margin.

"did you get his hight . . .   and
aproxemete age?"

i look cearfully at the new mister
gorf.

"he was sitting down, so i didn't
see how tall he was, but he lookt like
the sort of person who gets smaller as
they stand up."

"smaller as they stand up?"

"yes, you know, they have to sort of
hop down, like as if they are a bird on a
perch . . .   so who knows how little he
really is. youed have to see him walking
about to judge his real hight. but he
had a short clippt mustash, graying at
the tips. sort of salt and peppery. a bit
like a badger."

the new mister gorf rites a few more

lines in his ledger then bangs it shut
and tells me to go and sit down again.
"and be sure to report anything else that
comes to mind over the course of the
day." he adds with a fox's grin.

i nod and turn back towards the
busted chairs, smiling to myself on
having made such a good impression on my
very 1st morning.

besides, if he thinks that i
dont know when somone is patronising
me, then he is sorly mistaken. for all
his officeious note taking i would be
suprized if there is no investigation
into the missdaminas being played out
daily at the main gate.

i run my fingers along the cast
iron radiator and feel its teppid warmth
speaking to me thru the chipped, gray
paint. i have a real desire to touch
things and waigh them in my hands. this
time i really do go and sit down. i look
about that depressing cabin racking my
brains for clues that mite hint at the
gate mans identity. suddenly i remember
that he wore a ring.

"he was marrid!" i cry, jumping to
my feet. "he had a wedding ring on his
finger! . . . and medal ribons on his
chest . . ."

the new mister gorf looks across to
me with a cold blank stair.

"i'd say he was at least 75, if not

90." i add, firmly, befor sitting down
again and chew on my toung in thort. to
be precise the gray of the radiators is
more of a duck egg green, not unlike the
underside of a spitfire.

this new mister gorf finnaly puts
his pencil down, stretches out his
shoulder, puts his fury backed hands on
his thighs and springs into action. he
gets up and tells me to follow him.

i watch his shirt collar gently
throttling his neck as we head off across
the yard, at the bottom of the quadrangle
is a grass green painted nissen hut. he
ushers me in side.

theres a rush of hot air and smoke
that hits you right in the kisser as
you duck inside. theres a hole gang sat
there scoffing toast and necking tea. in
this style i truly enter the hallowed
relm of werking men. once they see the
door flung open it goes dead quite. even
the ones chewing the cud are caught mid
swallow and peer bug-eyed over the tops
of their tin mugs at us. only its not me
they'er looking at, its the new mister
gorf. most everybody's smoking and one
fellow is cooking up bacon on a charlie
nobel. he's the last to look up and is
caught there frozen, with the face of a
deformed chimpanzi.

gorf tells them all to carry on,
but they dont. to be honest, its not
quite the done thing: a brass neck coming

waltzing in during breakfast. before they stopped chewing you could see rite into their mouth: denturs and toast.

gorf calls out to one old lag, sat on his tod in the corner, crumbling a stock cube into a tin mug of hot water.

"heres your lad, bill."

bill pulls himself out of his arm chair, puts down his mug, and waddles over, brushing his hands on his overalls.

"this is mister cubitt. youre his apprentice. what do you think bill, will he measur up?"

bill looks me up and down. "that all depends, dosnt it, mister brightstone. theres not much meat on him, thou."

"put him to werk and your'll build him up."

"he'll do, i spose."

"he'll need boots mind. you cant have him out on site in those plimpsouls."

bill looks dubiously down at my bumper boots. "mister brightstones rite, your'll lose your toes, lad. does he have tools, mister brightstone?"

"off course he has tools, cubitt, what do you think we are. ile issue a chit for tools 1st thing tommorow, but its unlikely they'll be any in the store.

not masonry tools anyway. its a matter of finding a supplier."

"thats all well and good, mister brightstone, but how am i supposed to train a lad without the correct tools of the trade?"

"your'll have to make do, cubitt, make do and mend, as they say. meanwhile they'er on order."

"so next week then?"

"just as soon as we find a supplier."

"well they'er either on order or they'er not," mutters the one called bill.

"dont make problems, cubitt, there'll be by the end of the week. you take my word for it."

and this mister gorf come brightstone, backs out the caboos and leaves the door swinging.

bill walks over and closes it. "born in a fucking barn was he!" and immediately the place starts humming again. "you come with me lad. whats your name? . . . gustov? thats a funny one, what are you, an f-ing russen count?"

"its a family name."

"listen, you dont want to fall for old springheel jacks baloney," he nods

towards the door. "full of it, he is!
management always are! you mark my words:
there are no tools! ordered them? ordered
them my f-ing arse! you sit here and have
your breakfast. you've got tea? good.
come an sit down. this heres brincat."

a wirey youth crawls out from under
a bench.

"brincats my labourer. this heres .
. . gustov!"

brincat has small, sharp teeth and
his ears are tucked back like a ferrits.
i hold out my hand to shake his paw but
he just curls his lip and looks away in
disgust.

"would you belive it, brincat . .
. ive got an apprentice. 45 years ive
been here and never had an apprentice. f-
knows what im going to do with you!"

brincat sneers his yellow eyes.

"brincat escaped off the hulks,
thats how comes i own him. he's gone
ferrel like the dockyard cat. i said, you
live in the wood pile with the cats, dont
you, you convict!"

brincat curles his lip.

"dont you take no notice of him,
gustov. he's jellouse thats all. i said
your jellouse, arnt you brincat! i said
your not used to the ways of nobility!"

and bill roll's his eyes at me. this

must be one of the famouse dockyard jokes
ive been told to be on the look out for.

"no, brincats a good lad. though
he's not officially here, if you get my
drift. i had to get the bilboes cut off
him, over at the smithys. mums the word!"
bill taps his brezzer. "almost drowned
in the mud befor we pulled him out. 2
days and nites on the marsh. i said, you
almost drownded in the mud, didn't you,
you bin mounger!"

brincat gives a very cunning smile
and extracts, a small root vegtible
from his overalls pocket and feeds it
too something hiding inside his sacking
shirt.

*   *   *

i have decided to give myself a good
talking too and stop all this judging of
my fellow werkers, as if i am some sort
of god sat upon a mountain top with the
rite to fling lighting bolts into peoples
faces. no, its time to get into 'the
rythem of things'.

yes, that the phrase ive been
serching for all these years, 'the rythem
of things'. in just such a way i will
march into the werking life and make a
success of life.

that morning a tall, younger man, wearing
sideburns and a navy pinstriped suit was
talking to a short, rotund older man,
dressed in dusty blue overalls and a gray
cloth cap, a squall was blowing in across
the estuary.

the tall younger man, who
insidently, is hatless, gesticulates,
and explains something of the upmost
importence to the short, older man, who
is looking away almost notcholently,
stairing out over a stretch of enclosed
water, possably at a friget that is
moored there, or perhaps at a passing
gull that circels one of the crains
before alighting on the very fingertips
of its outstreatched arm.

the tall younger man is not entirley
sure that the short older man is exactly
listening. certenly he has incounted
dumb insolence from members of his class
before, but this devil is supposedly a
craftsman - and there fore elivated - and
should be on his side, at least to a
degree.

"but the bottom line is he cant be
on site wearing plimpsoles can he, bill!"

bill, putting his finger up the side
of his nose and sniffing the end of his
thumb, glances over at me, "ile have a
word with the lad, mister brightstone.

i stand off to the side, lift my foot and examin the sole of my bumper boots. theres a hole worn quite thru, my socks got all wet and you can see the tip of a toe, riggling in there.

springheel finishes his sermon and takes off, his head bobbing up and down like a rocking horse. bill mosses back over.

"lets get inside out of this blooming monsoon."

we go and sit in a corner of the caboos.

"rite, gustov, no more messing, we need to get you some werk boots."

"ive got these." i shoot my foot out and show him my bumper boots.

"yes, very nice. look, ive had springheel on my back all morning and im sick of seeing his mopey old mug on a stick. now theres a shop over the ways, next to riveters. its open dinner times, you fire your arse over there and buy yourself some safety boots."

"but im allright with these."

"thats what im telling you: your'll loose your toe if you drop a lump of rock on those dainty slippers!"

"they'er pretty strong."

"they'er bleeding plimpsoles with

holes in!"

"well i havent dropped anything on
my foot yet." i reason with him.

"you heard what old springheel said
- if your on site you need steelies."

"but these are comfortable."

"have they got steal toecaps?"

"no," i look at old bill with
his massive hooter taking up half of
his face, "mister brightstone was only
wearing shoes," i say hopfully.

"mister brightstone? dont call that
cows son mister."

"you did."

"only to his face. that ponce is
springheel jack to you."

i take a breath, "well, springheel
jack was only wearing shoes."

bill survays me wearily, "there not
ordinary shoes, they've got steel toecaps
as well."

"really?"

"of course they have. they'er just
the executive version, thats all."

"couldnt i get a pair of those?"

"only our manigment wear those.
we'er werkers, not ponces. werkers wear

thunder boots."

i look down and drag the left toe of
my plimpsoul thru a little pool of oil.

"listen up, gustov: bottom line
- you cant go skipping about in bluddy
ballet slippers. besides, old springheels
clocked you now, so its too late. plus
its against the safty reg's. you have to
wear steelies and thats it. period!"

"how much do they cost?"

"all prices. not much. i dont know,
a couple of quid, maybe. you'll get the
yard discount. so there cheeper than on
the outside."

"i spose i could. next week, when i
get payed."

"next week! . . . what size are
you?"

"8's."

"8's? well thats easy. ive got an
old pair in my donkey box. they'er not
much to look at but they'll pass muster,
till you get your pay check."

＊   ＊   ＊

next morning bill comes in and drops a
pair of old black bananas on the trestle

table infront of me.

"there you go, twinkele toes."

they clang as they hit the wood. i
put down my cheese sandwich and examin
them. they are pretty hard and stiff, and
theres some white mould growing on them
its also difficult to tell which foot is
which.

"dont get sniffy. that was the
style back then. they didnt bother with
left or rite. but i think this one's the
rite, the toe caps more mashed up, as i
remember."

i hold them up. so, the rite foot
is the one all twisted in on itself with
the toung like a pice of fosselised
cardboard.

"all they need is a bit of dubbin
on them - that'll soften 'em up lovely.
and ive got some string you can use for
laces."

bill really is doing his best to
jolly these boots up.

i turn the boot in my hand,
examining the soles, i can see that they
were once, in their long and illusterious
history, a pair of football boots.

"have these got steel toecaps?"

bill takes the boots from my hands,
"not exactly," he says deffencivly, "but
they look like they mite have - which

118

is better than nout. at least they'll
be keeping old springheel jack off your
back. look, you dont have to bleeding
wear 'em. ile bung 'em back in my donkey
box, shall i?" and bill turns as if to
leave.

i reach out to grab them back. "no,
i like them. honestly . . . they'er good
. . . like you say: take the studds off,
stich up this loose sole, put some string
in the lace holes and the'll be good as
new."

bill looks at me dubiously.

"you can fork out 3 nicker on a new
pair if your going to be picky about it."

"no, these will do fine . . . till
i get my pay check . . . i mean they'er
great, of course they'er a bit outdated,
but the old styles are all coming back
again. of course, its a bit difficult to
imagine them being at all comfortable,
but beggers cant be choosers. its just
a matter of werking out which foot is
which, thou i suppose that dosnt really
matter, ile soon wear them in." i smile
to reassure him. "thank you very much,
they'er great," i underline it.

"you go and bung 'em on then."

i sit and unlace my bumper boots and
try poking my toes into the hard jaws of
those viciouse boots.

it really is like trying to force

your foot into a paire of coconut shells.
the ankles seam to have curled in on
themselfs and hardened up somewhat. if
you prize them open with both hands
theres just time to slip your toes in
before the jaws snaps shut again, like a
deep sea clam. at last i stamp my foot
in, stand and clunk across the concreat
floor.

"he wont be scoring any goals in
them beatlecrushers!" jests one old
lag in a hat made entirely of sparrow
feathers.

"you leave him be, dicky bird. a
spot of dubbin and they'll be rite as 9
pence."

bill opens the door and i clonk off
after him.

※   ※   ※

outside bill pulls his cap on, hands me
a cloath tool roll, climbs on his old
bone shaker and wobbels off into the icy
drizzel.

"come on twinkle-toes put your best
foot forward."

the idear is that i have to trot
along behind, lugging the tool bag.

bill weaves his way between the

dock and the rail tracks, shouting
encouragment. rite away im out of puff
and have to spit. i look down at my feet
hitting the cobbles. the crains archimg
above me, some kissing the low scudding
clouds, whilest others dip their noses
into the oily waters.

bill looks over his shoulder to make
sure im still following him, swurves and
nearly drives into the oggin.

i do my best to keep up but the
boots cut into my ankles and i have to
hobble along sidways. also, the leather
studs on my boots keep skiding off the
cobbles and no matter which sholder you
carry the toolbag on it cuts into it.

bill is getting further and further
away. finnaly i have to drop the tools
on the deck and take a breather. way off
in the distence bill pulls up, turns and
shouts. i here him, way off.

"come on cupid, wake up, get your
arse in gear!"

i take a deep breath, lift the tool
bag to my least painfull shoulder and
dash on again, my boots clanging on the
rails, slipping this way and that. im
almost up level with bill when he stands
on the peddles and his off again, his
knees sticking out like a beetle.

i have to put on an extra spurt to
try to keep up, then one of the boots
flys off and i trip and fall arse over

121

tit. bill comes back and circles round
me.

"mind you look after them boots - i
scored a hat trick in them. luton rec,
1936 against the sappers. i put one past
nobby clark on the full time whistle,
and nobby clark was the best golie the
sappers ever fielded."

and with that bill straightens the
handle bars and is off again. i lean on
my elbow and whatch him go - rite the
ways down to the end of the warf, then
round the outer basin, to the bulls nose.
i see him teetering along the sea wall, a
flock of seagulls mobbing him.

when i finnaly walk into camp bill
is already sat supping a brew under an
awning beside the engin room.

"ah, the return of the prodigal
son."

i drop the tool bag and sit on a
lump of rock. my feet are like two hot
saussages.

"pick those up! - you dont drop
tools. tools are your lively hood! you
protect your tools before you protect
yourself. whats the 1st thing a rifel man
does when he stops marching?"

i shrug.

"he cleans his rifle, even befor he
eats his dinner. well thats the same for
you."

i pick the tools up and wearily look
for somewhere to place them.

"come on, give us 'em here. we may
as well get you started."

bill yanks the string and unrolls
the tools on the deck. for such precious
items all of them look pretty rusted up.

bill pulls out a claw and part of
the canvas comes away with it. he 'har's
on the handle and buffs it on the bib
of his overalls. "you dont get quality
like this anymore, oh no. these were hand
forged in blighty, none of your indian
rubbish. okay, they'er a bit rusty, but
nothing that a drop of oil and a bit
of elbow greece wont sort out. look at
that!" and he holds a twisted lump of
metal up to the lite, "good as new!"

bill slings the claw down and rolls
up a snout.

a wisp of smoke goes straight into
his eye. "you want some ticklers?" bill
offers me the tin. i shake my head. "good
for you. bludy stupid habit."

he blinks and rubs at it and a
little tear makes a path-way thru the
grime.

"i think im going to smoke a pipe."

"a pipe?"

"a clay one."

bill rubs his hands together,
massive fingers, flattening out towards
the ends, the nails shattered. "really,
a clay one? are you sure? my great
granddad smoked one of those - died of
cancer of the lip. a black spot. it grew
and grew. did i tell you that he was at
trafalga, on the tamirare? they built her
here. and the victory, of course." bill
takes another puff, picks at a strand of
tickler on his ovealls leg and puts it in
his mouth. "powder monkey he was, lived
till he was 106."

"now look, you see that there, what
you've parked your aris on? portland
stone, that is. it dosnt come more common
than that. you know the town hall?"

i nod.

"and the statue of genral gorden?"

i look at bill. im not really sure
what his on about.

"sat on his camel. up the sappers
baracks. the big blinking thing with a
hump! you walk past it every day."

"yes," i say uncertenly.

"well, its not made of re-inforced
concreat, is it? that means someone had
to carve it, with these!" and he holds up
his busted old mitts. "we're craftsmen
and dont let nobody tell you different.
you are an apprentice stonemason: be
proud of that title. carving stones isnt

some 3ruppeny 'appny trade, its a craft.
we'er not making garden gnomes, are we?
- no, i should think not."

bill takes a long drag, and starts
hacking up his guts. he buggs his eyes
and stairs at me with a flicker of fear.

"f- mine!" he bangs his chest and
exmins the end of his roll-up before
taking another lungfull and spitting a
golden oyster.

"if you dont have respect for
yourself, no one else is going to have
respect for you, are they? shit, shit
shit!"

bill jumps to his feet brushing
some burning ashes from his lap. "so's,
its all happening today, aint it. now
where was i? oh, yes, my great granddad,
wilfred. he ended up in the yard, but
that was back in the day.

"between you and me the stonemasons
an endaged species. its a dying art . . .
but keep your nose clean, and who knows?"

bill lays his index up against his
great, blistered hooter, every pore a
black head.

and sat just either side of it
- his gray eyes, with the whites gone
yellowish and little threads of red. bill
winks at me. the lids come together,
and there you have it - a wink! that
makes me jump, i stand on something and

nearly slip. bill grabs me by my arm and steadies me.

"mind out or you'll wind up in the oggin. we wouldn't want to loose you on your first day, would we! that'd be some christening, wouldnt it?"

bill amuses himself. his pretty pleased with his joke and he looks around too shear it, but brincats nowhere to be seen and theres no one else to laugh with him.

"see what you tripped on? portland stone that is, the masons bread and butter." bill taps his ash at it.

i look down at this famouse portland stone of his. to tell the truth it looks like a lump of junk.

"rite, no more gassing, we cant sit about all day doing f-all, theres werk to be done. your going to knock that old lump of old rock into a perfict cube. can you do that for me? thats your 1st job. to help get your hand and eye in. then will start you on your triumphal arch. you see them little shells?"

i peer at the rock. of course i understand that it is sedimentary rock and could there fore have been the bed of an ancient ocian, but really, it has shells in it?

"shale! look at that one - a real corker! the bane of the stonemason!"

now i see a little line thru the
rock - yes, the edges of ancient cockle
shells. a couple of solitary fellows and
a great big one, thumb nail sized.

"you'll learn all about him soon
enough. he'll blunt your chisels for
you, no mistake. go on, feel it, dont be
afraid of it, it wont bite you!"

i run my fingertips over the face
of the stone. its like reading brail.
smooth rock, then a lump and a little row
of pips with a little depression either
side. a triumph of prehistory: the bane
of the stonemason: a cute shell.

"okay, get started. theres no time
like the present."

i pick up the mallet and give the
chisel an experimental wack. bill holds
his hand up. "hold on, hold on, let the
dog see the rabbit. cricky, your'll put
us all to shame. we'll brew up 1st have a
snout, 'n' ponder it over."

⁜   ⁜   ⁜

after tea bill gets me to lift the rock
up onto an old sand bag, and after re-
itterating how rubbish the stone is, sets
me to chipping whilst he nurses his
tobbaco tin.

every now and then he opens his

eyes and calls some encouragment before sparking up and nodding off again.

his head lolls to one side, his toung comes out and all in all does a very fair impression of a dying dog. then theres an almighty snore and he jerks awake with a start.

"i was away there, boy. was i snoring?

"no, i never was. really? yes, i heard myself. well, wheres the harm? i had one eye open. i was just catching up, thats all. thats 15 winks and 25 to go.

"listen, one more thing, if you here 3 short taps of a hammer, followed by 3 long taps, followed by 3 short taps, thats the signel that springheel jacks is on the warpath. you hear 'tap-tap-tap, tap . . . tap . . . tap, tap-tap-tap' then you give me a nudge, rite. you got that? i can rely on you? now, lets check your angles so i can get some shut eye."

bill grabs the steel ruler, gets on down on his knees, holds it across the face of the stone and squints. "oh my gawd, look at that! its like a blinking roller coster ride! up hill, down hill."

the game is, if you can see lite under the ruler, then your eyes are bent and you cant carve for toffees.

"i shouldn't be able to pass a cigarette paper between the edge of this

ruler and the face of that stone. now,
look, gustov, you could get an f-ing
double decker bus under there, lad! thats
a mess . . . and thats a mess . . . and .
. . thats a mess to. not at any one point
should i be able to see daylite. its all
rubbish. well, your'll just have to start
over."

bill goes back over to his lump of
wood, parks his arse and makes himself
comfy. "you call me when you've got it
sorted. and remember, you hear 'tap-tap-
tap, tap . . . tap . . . tap, tap-tap-
tap' and you wake me up. pronto."

theres plenty of powder flying
about, starting with the most vicious
claw chisel, rite down to scouring the
surfiss with a piece of superfine sand-
stone. but to be honest, my heart wasnt
really in it from the outset.

yes, the stone game left me cold.
the little pieces of shale didnt like me
and i didn't like them, either.

you have to somehow become friends;
to learn to plecate their idocincrasitys,
and have them to come and love and obay
you.

just when you think that your
home and dry, you catch a crab with
your chisel and whoops! a great yawning
hole, and its back to re-working the
entire surface with the claw chisel from
scratch.

i keep hacking away and by the time bill wakes up again the cube has pretty much shrunk up and disappeared. he rubs his peepers, yawns, gets up and peers around looking for my block.

"christ, that stone was 1/2 a hundred waight when you started, now its all arisings. have you done a vanishing trick?" bill brushes the fag ashe off his bib. of course he is exaggerating, somewhat.

he goes and stands in the doorway.

"my, look at that sky. that dont look very promising, dose it, it'll be pouring by 2, you mark my words, we're in for a deluge!"

with that bill settles back down on his lump of wood and pulls his cap over his eyes.

      *   *   *

say what you like, but the werking life is full and vigerious. it is certenly not for the artistickly weak and namby-pamby.

and even if not so very much is expected of us, we still neather-the-less have to pry ourselfs out of our wank pits in the mornings and brush our own teeth till our gums bleed. neither do we have 'a man' stood to attenstion at the foot

130

of our beds, waighting to sponge us down,
dress us in silken finery then dust us
with apples with cinimon.

also, missing from the menue is
a horse and carrage drawn up on our
doorsteps, champing at the bit to wisk us
off to some weding-cake shaped mansion,
chock-full of high brested women,
masterbateing us into bone china teacups
whilest breast feeding us and alternately
offering us roasted humming-birds off
sharpend daggers.

true, my mother does bring me tea
in bed on these cold, dark mornings. and
she makes my sandwiches and ensures that
i leave the house on time to catch the
dockyard bus, but it is an exaggeration
to say that 'i get treated like a bludy
lord', or that i 'use my mother like
a bludy door mat!' as my father has
surgested.

"your abusing my facilitys!" he
speaks at me, on one of his rare visits.

i look at the back of his head as he
heads off upstairs to collect some clean
shirts and collars before telling mother
that she dosnt know how to press a pair
of trousers properly. a quick circit of
the garden to check up on dropped litter
and then hes off up the smoke again, in
his taxi, quick as greeced litning.

i have learned my lesson in regard
to the ways of taxi drivers.

no, we oxen desend on the dockyard
not by choffered limosines or over-priced
taxi cabs, but by pushbike and bus, and
of course shankes poney.

not that there is anything to
complain about once youve bitten the
bullit and emursed yourself fully into
the world of hard, uncearing, spitting
- then men all sorts of wonderful vistas
open up before your very eyes.

yes, what a playground the world has
become since i dont have to go to skool.

dinner times i borrow bills yard
bike and go off on little excursions
round the sea wall. it gets quite blowy
up there, you really have to lean into
the gale or it will push you off and help
you say hello to the concreat.

on one side you look down on the
slate gray river, chock full with mud,
and on the other lies a vast, waist land,
shrouded in mist. discarded rocks lie
scattered about like busted teeth amongst
flouresant pools of bubbling chemicals.
here, a broken mast off an ancent war
ship juts at an acute angle, there lies
a rusting anchor, maybe left over from
the dutch raid. and all of it is thrown
hither and thither, in natures scrap
yard.

someone happening across this
twist in the river for the 1st time mite
wonder why they call this 'the island'.
supposedly, before the convicts dug out

the basins, it really was one. but that
was way back in the days of missery, as
you can cycle out here nowadays without
so much as getting your tyers wet.

i jump off, lift the bike down the
sea wall and free-wheel it thru the bushs
into a little clearing.

the brambles and blackthorn grow
extra tall and thick round these parts on
account of the nuklia sludge they dump
out here on the qt. really, a bramble
bush growing as thick as your arm with
glowing blackberrys and throrns the size
of butchers hooks? thats an exaggeration
but still it cant be naturel.

but once your below the sea wall,
and out of the wind, and the sun peeps
thru and touches you with its healing
rays, then you have to conclude that this
is not so shabby a spot, as far as nuclia
swamps go. theres even some eagle sized
bull finches larking about in the bushes.

i hang my bag of mismatched tools
on a convenient nail and carry on carving
my sculpture of red cloud into a lump of
discarded lintel thats stood on end in
the mud like a totem-pole.

after 10 minits knocking up powder
i sling down my wormy old malet and blunt
chisil and take a nibble on a cheese
sandwich.

its quite remarkable that dust and
arisings would want to find their way

into every hidden crevis of a fellows
body. thru 3 layers of cloathing,
and rite into the center of a cheese
sandwich, even.

i leave a few crusts for the giant
dicky birds, add the nostrel to my
carving, then its time to head back.

i hike bills old bone-shaker up onto
the seawall, lean over the handle bars,
feed it a sugar lump and pat its metal
neck.

as theres no chain guard i tuck my
overall bottoms into my socks and rattle
off. call me old fashioned, but it really
wouldnt hurt to have some brakes and
tyers on something called a bike.

as you come round the last stretch
of the wilderness, you get a clear view
of the open river. i have my neck pretty
much shrunk back into my body as the
north wind is after it, but here i stand
on the peddles and streatch it out a bit.
theres quite a crowd gathered on the
bulls-nose, shading their eyes, gawping
into the distence. theres something big
out there on the river.

this is how it goes: its all peace
and tranquility, but once us skivers get
wind theres an 'appny dip' coming in,
everyone downs tools and scampers over
to the edge to have a looksy. mugs of
pefickly good tea get left to go stone
cold and delicious marmite sandwiches
curl up in the salt wind and get nicked

by maureding seagulls. from all over theres a drumming of boots as the werk force makes a dash for the bulls nose.

i can see that they've already got the caisson open on the werking lock, so i stand in the pedels and cycle like the devil.

what ever it is, its chucking up a hefty bow wave. the wash surges against the opestite bank and bellow me it sounds as it slaps into the sea wall, chucking up a salty spray that the wind grabs and flings in your face.

i have to cross the far caisson at full pelt, before they stop the traffic and im left stranded. i skid to a stop and lean the bike against the wall of the engin room. bills no where to be seen, nor brincat, nor his ferrit for that matter. they must already be on quay side, getting the measure.

i push thru the crowd. some of these loafers even have jobs to do: manhandling the hawsers and closing the road. theres the pumps to operate as well. but the gawpers out number the werkers 20 to 1.

she comes in at full tilt, a black pig, waves almost up to the conning tower.

the brave commander stands with his muscular thighs well braced. hes having a whale of a time up there, showing off his peaked cap and shouting orders thru his loud hailer.

all the matlos dashing about,
chucking springlines this way and that.

i talk as if the commander is just
sitting next to us but in truth you can
scearsly see him, only a speck with a hat
and some speggeti, almost out of sight,
reduced by distance, the perspective of
the quayside.

somone grabs me from behind so's i
jump and nearly fall in. i turn round.
its brincat.

"where you been? bills been looking
all over for you!"

"i was carving."

"carving! theres fucking werk to do,
boy!"

he holds me with his small, worried
eyes. really, his whole forehead wrinkles
up and his lips curl to meet his pointy
nose.

i look away. "bill said i could go
for 1/2 an hour."

"bill said, bill said! you aint got
special privleges just cos your the new
fucking apperntice. if i tells you to do
something, you fucking well has to do it.
you ask bill, he'll tell you. you do as i
say round here, boy!"

brincats pet weasel sticks its nose

out of his fearnaught and nudges his
chin. brincat, kisses its nose, rumeges
thru his pockets and holds a small fish
head between his thumb and forefinger.
"furrycat needs his grub!" he tells me,
instructionally.

i watch as furrycats small blueish
toung comes out and licks at the fish
skin, before snapping it down with its
sharp fangs. brincat looks back up at
me.

"you cant just go fucking off like a
cunt, no matter what bill says."

then bill shows up and brincat
pretends to be giving me a piece of
brotherly advise.

"any way, like i was saying, dont go
to near the edge, or mister cubitt will
be blaming us for you falling in!"

bill shines his eyes at brincat.

"you still got that bleeding ferrit
stinking up the f-ing place . . . you
see that?" bill nods to the sub, "thats
the winston churchill, she is. improved
valiant class. my mate werked on the
generator when she was in the nuclia."

brincat looks it over, "how do they
see under water, then?"

"what do you mean, how do they see
under the f-ing water?"

"well if it aint got no portholes,

hows it know not to bump into stuff?"

"because its got a bleeding periscope and a sonar."

"that mite be, but hows it know its not going to hit an iceburg?"

"well there arnt any f-ing iceburgs on the medway are there, so its not a concern."

"maybe it uses feelers," i surgest.

brincat looks at me.

"like a beetle. or one of those fish, a barble."

"what?"

"a barbel, they've got barbels - dangly bits round their top lips. you know, for feeling in the dark."

"is he taking the piss out of us!"

bill puts his spade up in the air. "you, less of the langwige! and you, stop winding him up."

"brincat looks bitterly at bill, "'e can say what 'e wants now 'es your apprentice. but i was here 1st, and if he wants some fucking shirts off ile give him fucking shirts off! fucking apprentice. whats he know about fucking ships!"

"1stly a submarin is a boat, not

a ship. and 2ndly, she needs to tie
up sharpish or she'll smack into that
caisson and that'll be another saga for
muggings to sort out."

the commander peers down from
the conning tower. theres allsorts of
currents sloshing about, dragging the
sub this way and that. just because hes
managed not to crunch into the seawall
dosnt mean that its time to put his feet
up and start puffing on his pipe.

"oh my gawd," crys bill, covering
his eyes with his handkerchief, "look at
him. he needs to make his bleeding mind
up. rite on the agony strokes and hes
gone changed his mind! i wouldnt let him
steer a lawn mower let alone put him in
charge of a black pig. if he takes out
that other caisson an' all, well, they
may as well invite old breshnev to nuke
the yard! you know we'er 3rd on the list
dont you? london 1st, then its birmingham,
then us."

"what list?" asks brincat.

"the blowing us all to kingdom come
list," says bill.

just in time the commander jams her
full astern. the spring men jump in and
the air grows dark with hemp. the bow
lines are attached and some real wurl-
pools start up, sucking right down onto
the dockbed. a vortex of cockels and
mussels: bits of barnical mixed in with
the crabs and jellyfish.

we stand back and savour the stink.
bill shakes his head sorrowfully. it
really is as if the captain has let him
down personally.

"i dont know what the f-ing navys
coming too, drowning their own men, look
at those poor devils."

i hear what bills saying, but i see
nothing.

"looky yonder, and open your eys.
under the flags. 3 of 'em. fresh out of
davey jones locker! not up there, down
there! on the bleeding poop. 3 of 'em,
behind old brass neck."

bill wags his finger in their
direction. a truncheon waving thru the
sea air. a matlow with a rifel narrows
his eyes and looks daggers at bill. bill
stops pointing and clasps his hands
behind his back and nudges me, "take your
f-ing cap off!"

i doff my cap. brincats not wearing
one. i see what bills pointing at now: 3
bodys, bundled under some white ensigns.

"they were on manovers in the north
sea, playing at solders," whispers bill.
"those poor bleeders was on the fittleton
and got rammed by the mermaid, a thumping
great friget. drags their little mine
sweeper to the bottom of the oggin and
those poor devils never got out."

the corners of the flags flap in the

140

wind and i imagin the mad rush of water
filling their lungs, and then their souls
trapped under the black waves.

a hurse pulls up, followed by a
little fleet of black lemos and then the
admriel staff car. the admrils driver
jumps out and gallops round to open the
door for the boss, who steps out, his
chest sagging under 3 rows of medels. he
unbends and sticks his cocked hat on his
head, just like lord nelson.

a guard of matlows barge into us,
cleaning the way. we all have to back
off.

bill keeps up a running commentry
out the corner of his mouth. "look up,
here comes the top brass. and you see
that lot? they'er the relitives. see
them in the black vailes? they'er the
wives and mothers, and those must be the
children. they've pushed the boat out, if
your'll pardon the expression. that suit
must have cost a pretty penny. and is
that a tuxsido his wearing?

the relitives get out of the black
limos, white-faced, shaking hands with
the top brass. yes, a real admiral,
humbling himself. he has large, watery
eyes set on top of a pair of purplish
bags.

theres a euligy, but we cant hear
much of it from back here.

the flag dips to half mast and the
bugle sounds all forlorn.

we shuffle our feet and look away,
studying the churchill, lying their
waiting for the lock to fill up so's she
can mossy on into the basin. you here
the pumps cranking away and you know
that in its own way it is a perfictly
ordinary day, and later we will forget
all this, but not the crying ladys and
the sullen faced children. they will have
to remember it forever.

a big lout pushes in front and i
have to stand on tiptoes. thats me all
over, curious as a kitten.

the wind continues to play tag with
the ensigns, teasing the corners, lifting
and dropping . . . we stand, dry-mouthed.

in point of fact we'er not morners,
but imposters. what we're standing here
for has naff all to do with showing our
last respects, we're solely here for the
horror show: to stand and gawp at death
from a safe distence, the cheerless
sun bleaching out our cold faces. yes,
we want to get as close to the edge as
possible, without actually falling in.
and the corpses lieing there, trussed
up round and bloated, a whole barrel of
saltwater slopping around in their dead
guts? they are a diversion from the dayly
grind; to mention in passing in cheap
public houses and trashy novels.

a sudden gust of wind lifts a flag

clean off the most bloated corps. it
is as if the wind wants to molest his
salt encrusted face for one last time,
who knows, prehaps the corps demanded
this favour of the wind and being of an
obliging mind the wind agreed to kiss his
cheek one last time.

a little gasp goes up, but not
of horror but of discontentment: there
is not a green mottled corpse lying
prostrate, just a misshapen blimp swathed
in polythene sheeting. no, we gate
crashers don't get our money's worth at
all, and are cheated of a glimpse of the
smiling face of king death.

actually, we're incredulous.

we hear the bugler playing the last
post, then theres 3 minutes silence.

its time for us to get lost. the
crowd starts breaking up and drifts off
like lumps of ice. me 'n' bill pick our
way back to the engin house, brincat
follows on holding furrycat to his cheek.

the dredger, just of shore, starts
up again.

diddnt i tell you about it? a whole
crane chained to a raft - a kind of
floating platform, barge-like, a lump of
steel realy - still with the caterpillar
tracks on. he sits there in his cab, a
little figure at sea, working his levers
. . . mobbed by seagulls, their screams
fill the air, competing with his engine.

it whines in agony . . . he's caught
something big, it almost pulls him in
with it. then the jaws break free of the
waves, streaming seaweed and black mud
from between its iron teeth. the great
cycle of life: the resettlement of silt.

bill parks his arse and tells me to
nip to the tea fanny.

a couple of card games start up and
the welders spark up their blue torches.
you have too look away or damage your
eyes for life.

i bring bill his mug. we all need
the rest, its been a hard day.

brincat pipes up, "did you see him?
the fat barstard? . . . when the flag
lifted up . . . had a face like a mouldy
lump o' mouse meat."

"mouse meat?" i ask.

"cheese," says bill stareing into
his mug. i get the message, look down and
dunk a digestive biscit.

"oi, give us one of those nibby's
for furrycat." and brincat reaches over
and snatches a digestive from my hand
and rite on cue furrycat pops his head
out of brincats fearnaught, twitching his
nose and showing his sharp little teeth.
brincat holds the nibby up, just out of
furrycats reach.

furrycat lifts his front paws,

crouches, then springs into the air just missing brincats fingers, "ouch!"

"ive told you that f-ing animal belongs in a bleeding cage!" bill turns to me, "that little barstard latched onto my finger once. i had to hold the little f-ing barstard under water for 5 minits for it would let go. clamped on, it was, like a c - tart!"

"its not his fault. furrycat didn't mean no harm, did you." simpers brincat.

"i had to near drown the barstard to make it let go! look theres the scar. bit clean thru to the bone, it did."

brincat nurses furrycat to his chest, "dont listen to the crazy man," and holds a piece of nibber between his lips and feeds it to furrycat, for all the world like a mother mink feeding its baby a mashed up beatle.

chapter 7

a ferrit-faced youth could be seen in
the early moring lite, dangling a piece
of bent wire from a string into the oily
water of the basin 20 feet bellow.

the winter sunlite is harsh and
makes the youth squint the sandy coloured
lashes of his small eyes.

likewise a blond polecat pokes
its nose from the ferrit faced youths
fearnaught. the polecat sniffs the cold
air, then hops down onto the dockside and
nibbels at a pile of jellyfish laying
there, dying in the dust.

bellow, 7veral more jellyfish can
be seen lapping alongside the dock wall.
the ferrit-faced youth swings his hook,
draging it thru the brakish water, and
all the while he is muttering under his
breath, coxing them onto the hook.

"come on . . . you fucking jellys .
. . get on the hook for daddy."

and he jerks the string rythmicly,
snaging a jellyfish which he lifts clear
of the water. he reaches out to draw
the line in with his free hand and the
bent wire rips free off the mass and 2
quithering sections of the jellyfish drop
back into the basin, to slide benieth the
small wavlets and sink out of site.

146

"fuck it!"

the ferrit faced youth stairs
angrily at the waters bellow.

*   *   *

by the breath rising up from under the
knitted blanket it is possible to decern
that the bed is inhabited.

in the widow hang a pair of mothy,
thread-bare curtens doing little to keep
the blueish morning lite from the tiny
room. the bedroom was icy cold.

on close inspection tufts of
blondish hair can be seen sproutting
there on the ticking pillow case.

the window itself glazed with a thin
sheet of ice.

many posters crowd those narrow
walls, which can scearlsly accomidate the
tiny single bed and absurd gerry-built
wardrobe, which takes 1/2 the room.

your country needs you, proclaimes
lord kitchener, pointing a white gloved
hand at your nose.

jesus saves, voices another, which
sports a badly drawn cartoon of christ,
grimly shoudering his cross and clasping
a piggy bank to his breast.

jimi plays berckly is the message on
the poster, badly pasted to the inside of
the closed door.

all of these master pices are
framed, as it were, with cut-outs of
naked ladys of the past. sucking in their
guts, protruding their bristols and
stroking kittens; or fondling watering
cans; or holding tennis rackets; or stood
on step laders; or simmply caught in the
act of unclasping their braziars, but
always with big hair, big eyelashes,
pouting lips and no virginas.

the door opens and a 50 year old
women enters the gloom, clasping her
dressing gown about her.

"look at the time. your tea's stone
cold. are you awake? well, youed better
get up or your'll be late!"

of course, not every werking boy
gets brought tea in bed by his adoring
mother, and i should no doubt be
greatfull, despite the early houre.

my mother prods me. i lie there and
let her worry that im dead before finnaly
lifting the blanket and showing my mug.

"look, heres your tea. i brought
it in 1/2 an houre ago. its gone 6, you
know."

i sit up and look around me in shock
- can it really be that early? - then let
my head drop back onto the pillow.

"get up or your'll miss the bus."

and my mother backs out the room.

i listen out for her feet on the
stairs, then sip the cold tea and flex
my eyelids. it takes me another 6 or
7 attempts 'til i finally vow to stop
amusing myself and spring into that iced
room.

yes, theres ice on the inside of the
window, my tea is cold and we cant afford
to have the heating on as my mother is on
one of her 'economy drives' but is this
a reason to rite a novel that amounts to
a list of complaints? of course not, and
on the whole i am very happy and content
with my damp little corner that life has
allotted me.

i grab my trousers, climb in, button
up and go down stares, jumping the last 6
steps.

my mother hands me my tin of
sarnies, which i bung in my scran bag,
along with my book on fauvisim, sketch
book and an apple. thus equipt i head out
into the fog looking for my bus.

one last swig of tea befor i go,
then, and ile be off.

hundreds of us are heading for that
gate. my grandfather before me, reg, on
my mothers side, ive told you about him,
then his father william, his father befor
him, etc. a whole bevey of ghosts.

i go to muster - we get 6 minits lee as
we'er away from the main gate - i make it
with 45 seconds to spair, then push into
the caboos and sit down.

a small face peeps from out of
brincats fearnaught. brincat puts his
thumbs under furrycats armpits and lifts
him out. the more he lifts him the longer
furrycat gets, like an old ladys fur
muff. he plonks him down on the trestle
table, where he starts peeing.

the chief sherang bangs down his
cup. "oi, get that fucking carpet shark
off the fucking table and put it back in
its fucking cage! its stinking up the
whole caboos. and its unhighenic!"

"im just giving furrycat his
breakfast." and brincat mops at the
puddle of pee with his cuff.

"you heared me - off the table!" the
chief sherang points his eyes and rises
his finger.

"ralph has his cat in here," whines
brincat, "and he's allowed to draw in
here!" its true, im drawing the tea pot.

"i said off the table and out side,
and take the fucking carpet shark with
you!"

brincat scoops furrycat up into his

fearnaught and storms out letting the door bang behind him.

theres no sign of bill as yet.

i have a sip of tea and carry on drawing. i just get the spout done and start in drawing in an old fellow with a crusty claw holding onto a tin mug, when i hear bill coming; little wheezes, the shuffling of the pedals; a bike being rested up against the corrugated iron. then the door opens and in comes bills cap, he flings it across the room and it skids across the table.

"phew, im shagged! give us a mug of that char, gustov!"

i dip bills mug in the tea fanny and plonk it down in front of him. bill lifts it to his lips, sticks his nose in it, breathes through the steam clouds and sucks it down in one go. a purse of his lips and he drains the lot, sieving the leaves.

"ah, thats better!" he bangs his mug down lets out a little fart of hello and he settles himself in.

after breakfast, we cycle out round the sea wall to take a gander at my carvings.

in truth, i trot along behind whilest bill rattles along on his bare rims, pointing out the landmarks.

"thats where the dutch landed. well
somewhere over that a-ways . . . lower g
-, they reckon . . . . smashed thru the
chain across the river . . . paid someone
to let it go more like . . . treated
the locals better than our seaman, so
they say . . . proberby all bollox . . .
and that over there was the site of the
plague pits."

bill points and cycles along one
handed and almost topples. "this bleeding
wheels buckled have you been riding my
bike?"

i have to drop back a step as bill
drifts off across the path, his arse
showing, the top of both cheeks.

"they asked for volenteers from the
yard to fight the buggers . . . do you
know how many stepped forward?"

"3" i answer.

"3!" says bill, triumphantly, "you
know what that means?"

"dont volenteer?"

bill stops, puts his foot to the
ground, and looks at me.

"dont volenteer for anything! you
remember that, gustov, lad."

i nod.

with that bill lets his bike drop
to the ground.

"allrite curuthers, you lead the
way," and we wade off thru the giant
nettles.

"if you volunteer, your asking for
it in the neck. history will tell you
that, the whole story. everythings in
history. all the balls-ups."

i carry on nodding and saying 'yes'.

we come to the clearing.

bill shakes his hanky at a lump of
rock, parks his arse and goes for his
baccy tin, and out comes his flask. he
pours me a glug and laces them both with
a fist of rum.

"here, get that down you, that'll
thicken your toenails. nibber?"

bill takes out a 1/2 packet of
digestives and offers me one. he breaks
one over the packet: the scattering
of the crumbs, he taps it with his
forefinger and they come to rest. then
in it goes down his open trap. a little
ritual: the dunking of the digestive.

bill sits back and survays my
carvings, swallows, narrows his eyes and
picks at something right at the back of
his gob. he inserts a large, blunt finger
and fishes about in there, extracts
it and studies the tip, a fat knuckle
and some yellow scum under his nail.
he sucks it clean and looks up. "nah,
we cut in marble, an historical stone.

michelangelo, what did he carve in? - it
wasnt chalk, was it."

"no." i answer dutifully.

"absolutly rite it f-ing wasnt.
marble, thats the stuff: thats how i
was taught, back in the day: monumental
masonry. none of this portland rubbish!"

"is that carving gravestones?"

"monuments mostly, but you could say
that gravestones come into it but they'er
not the whole story.

"it was a different world 40 years
back now . . . going on 50, maybe . . .
anyway, donkys years back. you know that
statue of gordon? restoring that i was,
as a nipper. that was my apprenticeship,
when masonry was still a respected craft
and you could hold your head up high.
you had a trade under your belt, and not
just some run of the mill monkey trade,
either. artisan, you were. we weren't
treated like second rate labourers in
those days, no f-ing way! least of all
by university-boys, still wet behind the
bleeding ears, like old springheel jack.
mincing about with his soft hands." bill
leans forward and spits.

it never occured to me that
springheel had been to university, nor
that his hands mite be soft. certenly he
had sidburns.

"i didnt know mister brightstone

went to university."

"of course he went to f-ing
university! anyway, less of your 'mister
brightstone', i told you its springheel
jack to you. bouncing along like hes an
f-ing girl in a shampoo advert!"

"which university did he go to?"

"blowed if i know, but if he thinks
that he can send me down some sump
hole to machine bits off a granit slab
because some monkeys gone bent the bloody
caisson, hes got another think coming!"

bill stares contemptuiously into the
bewhiskered mush of my carving.

"who the hell is that ment to be?"
he asks moodily.

"its a reclining admiral."

bill shakes his head. "f- mine, hes
a miserable looking sod!"

"hes based on my father" i say
defensivly.

"sorry, no disrespect."

"do you think i should re-do the
epaulatts?"

bill shruggs. "you could do, i
spose. if you can be bothered. not that
theres much point."

"i thort it mite make him look more

like an admril, seeings hes not wearing a cock't hat."

bill nods thortfully. "trouble is, this stone, its junk. it wont take the detail. if you ask my candid oppinion you need to be werking in marbel. we didnt piddle around breaking rocks in my day."

"do you think we could get some marbel, then?"

"nah."

"maybe we could ask mister brightstone . . . i mean springheel jack?"

"springheel? he wouldnt no marble if it dropped on his foot. granit, thats as much as his brain can comprehend. and thats as much as yourll run into in the yard: granit, or a bit of portland, if your lucky. but marble? you can blinking whistle for it!"

bill rolls another snout. fills the fag paper with some crumbs, licks it and pinches it together. he sparks up and breaths out a stream of blue smoke. it really does smell like some king of tasty meals. he glances at me then back at my carving.

"im not saying nothing more or less, if you get my drift, than the obvious, gustov: if you treat stone - or shall we say marbel - with its due, then in all probobility it will be friendly back to

you. you can only hope. but if you dont
respect it, then the stone wont respect
you, will it . . . and mark my words, it
will become the masons worst enimy."

"any tom, dick or harry can lay
brick, gustov. granted, theres a few
wrinkles, but nothing a monkey cant be
taught in an afternoon. thats if anybody
could be bothered to teach a monkey
bricklaying, of course - har, har!

"everyone makes such a hoo-har
about building a little brick wall, but
the acroppolis isnt a brick wall, is it?
but to here this lot speak youed think
it sprouted up over nite, like a horse
mushroom."

you can see bills dentchers drop
each time he opens his mouth, and i
become mesmerized and forget to listen to
what it is his actually saying.

"you ask any man in the yard,
and they'll most likely tell you that
haydrens wall is made of bricks and re-
inforced concrete. and truth is, it may
as well be. did you know the romans
invented concrete?"

"sort of," i answer. "i used to do
some arciology."

bill looks at me askance. "so you
know it wasnt all marbel, then?"

"yes," i answer.

"well then, you know that even
when you do come across a bit of marble
in this country it will be to brittle,
and therefore unworkable. thats because
marble isn't suited to england, what with
its climatic variations, isnt it."

i nod.

"people look up to your
michelangelos, but what your average
college graduate will never get into
their thick skulls is that all stone is
basicly a natural barometer.

"its all very well crying and
making a song and dance about the buti
of marble, but what your college boy is
forgetting is that we live on a cold damp
island. we'er not on the bleeding medway
as in f-ing mediterainian, are we?

"occasionally we mite have a heat-
wave, granted, but on the whole the
summers a wash out. you tell me the
last time you had a suntan. you follow
my drift? it rains rite thru june, july
and august, then its autumn, and before
you know it its the big freeze, and we
wont see the sun for another 6 months.
and, if theres one thing marble wont
tollerate its cold and damp. it seizes
up and becomes arthritic and brittle. to
all intents and purposes its unworkable.
there you have it, the answer to your
riddle: wcv - weather and climatic
veriation. wcv, remember those 3 letters
and you wont go far rong.

"okay, your following me, but you try telling that to spingheel jack. that universty ponce is nothing but a charlatan! he dosnt know his jurassic from his precambrian . . . he hasnt had the training, and wheres he going to get it? 'cos i tell you, you cant learn it from books. springheels never so much as look't at a chisel, least of all belted one with a mallet. of course, the marbles f-ing unworkable, we aint living in pompeii, are we? a schoolboy could tell him as much!"

bill grinds out his dog end and starts rolling a fresh one.

"ah, but when the marble is freshly cut from the quarries of old carrara, thats a different kettle of fish altogether. its a joy to werk with - you can carve it with a pen knife. it doesnt flake or splinter, either. not the way it does in this damned climate. my goodness gracious no, it cuts like a mature cheddar!"

i sit and try and picture this cheesy marble of bills, but then he starts up again.

"the stonemasons worst enemy, wcv! hours of painstaking detail gone up in smoke! the finest most intricate gingerbread work, destroyed! rubbed out for good! in one frost! i dont even want to here about it. i know all there is to know about that fish, and ive had it up to here!"

bill glares at me, dareing me to
contradict him.

"can you even imagin the effect
of ice cristalls in a semi-porus
enviroment?"

i nod. of course i can imagin it
quite clearly, and in all sorts of ways.
mainly microscopicly. but the more i do
imagine it, the more complecated the
pictures in my mind become. "no," i
answer, "not really."

"it becomes totally unworkable!
splinters flying left rite and center!
slithers shooting out in all directions!"

bill aims a kick at my sculpture.

"portland is childs play. yes it
gets in your hair and jammed up your
crack, but marble? essentially the finner
flakes are mini stiletoes. they actually
cut and slice. your thumb, the back of
your hand, even your eyes. and you cant
go yanking those out by brute force. not
if you value your eyesight, you dont!
the trick is to pluck a single hair from
your head . . . like so. make a little
loop . . . like that, then hook it round
the spear of the marble and then ease
it out slowly . . . and i mean slowly
mind, becous you dont want to loose your
eyesite . . . ah, ha! an art in itself,
paid for with experience! but this stuff?
dont make me chuck up. stone? chalk more

like! only not half as useful! give me a
good bed of marble any day of the week!
oh! jesus h christ, my ticker!"

bill sloutches forward holding onto
his hart. i stand and look about the
bushes.

"shall i go and get some help?"

"nah! ile be allrite in a jiff.
just give us a swig of that tea! and put
another tot of rum in there for me, will
you gustov, lad. christ! . . . ah, yes .
. . mmm, thats better."

bill takes a long swig.

"whats the miniutes, gustov? did
you hear the cannon? i was away there .
. . i almost went off on one . . . come
on, lets get out of this swamp, you go
sitting around on cold rocks all day
you'll get piles! did i tell about my
gran? she got hers caught in the chain
of her tricycle and went clean over the
handle bars, i kid you not!"

we had the whole show pretty much to
ourselves out there, perched on the
tippy-tip of the bulls-nose. the sky
comes down to say hello and you peer thru
the swirles and eddies to the top-masts
of the little ships; and then the war
ships as well - their comings and goings.

everybody paddles past: mine
sweepers, frigets, a stumpy aircraft
carrier, all sorts emerging from the end
of the world, and then the sea birds as
well. a gull as big as an albotoss, hung
there in the sky by a wire. he moves his
head slightly and veers off down wind,
then holds there again, rite above me,
studying the deck for crusts and fish
heads.

a thousand commotions. the dredger
hauls out great jawfuls of black mud. the
man in the little cabin: you can just
make out his arms going, cranking the
leavers. theres a wiff of diesel and you
can just hear the genirator banging away.
little puffs of blue smoke going up like
a panting poney, then the crain swings
round and emptys another gobful into the
open topped barge alongside. you here a
distent clang and the crain swings round
and dives in for 2nds: the never ending
battle to keep the navigation channels
open.

naturally the whole place has its

own special arromer so your not just
seeing stuff but smelling it all at the
same time: oil, rot and brine.

just as its time to go i spot a
family of cormorants perched out on the
navigation bouys, hanging their wings
out to dry, so to speak. then off they
hop back in the oggin. they go down under
for a good 2 minits into that mud filled
world. i search the waters for their
snaking necks and it seams their gone for
good, then way out in mid stream i catch
a glimpse . . .

as i look many little feelings come
over me like ancient memorys. sometimes
its pleasent to feel so raw and alive
and then a feeling of great meloncolly
emerges and it feels barren and godless
to be stood out here on a concete pier,
embarking on life.

i thro the crusts of my cheese
sandwich to the water and the great gull
dives from the gray sky to scoop them up
in his mighty beak. i turn my shoulder
and go back to the pumping station.

bill's still sat on a lump of wood,
lent back agant the wall with a spotted
hanky draped over his face. he snatches
it away as i come in and pretends to be
wipeing his brow.

"all rite leonardo, where you been,
doing you drawing?"

"i was just watching stuff."

bill ajusts himself.

"your'll have to draw me. but not like this. with my best whistle on. not that it fits anymore. i kept it for best after i was de-mobed and never worn it since. whats the point, i dont go to church and i dont exactly werk in a bank, do i?"

bill winks at me. he's fagged. its all the talking. he drags himself to his feet.

"ile show you about, so's you know whats what. thats brincats hiding spot, under the box shed. you dont know thats there. if anyone asks you if you've never seen him, you haven't. you dont even know his name. thats his drinking bowl, and that sack hanging from the hook, thats where he keeps his stale crusts, so's the rats dont get 'em. remember - mums the word, rite!"

we carry on picking thru the debris and into the arear where men are actually werking. theres jagged shapes of metal everywhere and a whole little army removing and re-fixing. the fizz of welding torches, a man with bright ginger hair holds a mask to his face and the blue lite cuts rite through the steel, little balls of molton metal bounce onto the concreat floor, were they scurry along and turn charcole black.

"dont stair at it, you'll burn your retiners out! look, this is what i wanted to show you, down that hole."

theres a cut away in the concreat.
i peek in, but there's nothing in it.
i check in all the corners but its
absolutely empity.

"now how am i ment to get down there
and swing a hammer? f-ing sringheel jack.
"re-bed the cambers!" he say's. well,
there was nothing rong with 'em in the 1st
place, the tart! talk about make a saga!"

bill sticks out his left buttock and
farts.

"it was allright when they lifted
the f-ing caisson out, wasn't it! well
the camber hasent grown over nite, has
it? granite isn't mushrooms, is it? . .
. its the steal thats destorted, plane as
the nose on your face! so now muggings is
ment to get down on his hands a knees -
in that f-ing sump hole - and chisel away
like an f-ing navi, am i, just to cover
up their ball's-up? pardon me, but they
can blow that out their arse!"

the big problem, it seems, is that
the caisson wont fit into the camber
anymore. it was fine when they hoiseted
her out but now she's been 'all bolloxed
up'. after a million calculations, a
thousand fine atunements, the baby won't
get back into her cot.

the consensus is its all bills
fault. another two sixteenths of an inch
chisseld from the surface of the granite

floor of the camber and everything would
be snug and perfict.

"dont worry, the yards full of
experts who know nothing. yourll get
used to it. at least we get paid at the
end of the week, not like you, - your
one of the new mob - paid by check,
rite? fornightly? you do know that,
dontcha? well, we'er all old skool and
can draw our ackers from the pay point
on thursdays. any new 'un's - that
includes you - have to have an f-ing bank
account! thats very nice, they've got
you by the short and curlys. dont get me
rong, they asked us as well: 'do you want
your wage packet paid directly into a
bank account?' - 'no i f-ing well dont!'
i said. 'it will be more convient,'
they said. 'yes' i said, 'more bleeding
convenient for you!

"they'er f-ing full of it - and its
all bollox! its muggings who has to go
draw his money out, and the f-ing banks
arnt f-ing open after werk are they?
'your'll get a free check book,' they
said. 'i dont want a free f-ing check
book,' i said. 'i want dollar bills in
my back pocket, thank you!' dont worry,
your'll see."

i stand over the empty pit. its
more the line for a skilled labourer
with a power chissel, not a master mason
of bill's calibre: a man of yesteryear,
educated exclusively in marble.

"come on, lets go get a brew going. i dont like looking down that 'ole, it gives me the colly-wobbels."

bill spits his dog-end in the pit and sparks up a fresh one. he puffs out a lungful and coughs. he drags it up from deep down and spits a real glistner . . .

bill stands there for a moment, balancing on the edge, nodding his head in compleat agreement with himself, then suddenly pops his eyes and spouts red. a great jet of it. a beautiful plume goes up: arching scarlet against the sky. a look of surprise flashes across bills face, then up it goes! a ray of sun peeps out and catches it just as it reaches its apex. the globuels hanging there in mid-air, caught in time as it were, before the wind catches them and they spatter down in black clots in the dust.

bill tilts his head back, squeezing his neb with the hanky. "me doze." he explains, "a safety valve, der quack tells me . . . high blood pressure."

he dabs at his neb, red, swollen . . . he studies the cloth, a beautiful rose . . . a little string of snot. he re-wipes and pockets the package for safe keeping. the blud streams down his chin and covers his shirt front.

"dat's it. dat's stemmed der fucker!"

i come into the caboos next morning and
bills armchair is empty.

"its his blood pressure," springheel
tells me, "he mite be in later."

"what shall i do?" i ask.

"i dont know. tiddy up. whatever
werk mister cubitt has set you. you go
out on site and ile send someone over to
check on you this afternoon."

"ive got a rock im ment to make
into a cube, but bills tools are in his
donkey box."

"well im giving you permission to go
into mister cubitts donky box and borrow
his tools."

"he keeps it locked up."

"my, youre a problem maker, not a
problem solver, arnt you, claudius."

"i haven't got a key. i could do
some drawing," i say hopefully, "or go
home."

springheel holds me with a withering
look. i realise that i have said the rong
thing and indevour to make amends.

"maybe my tools have come in."

"i dont think they have arrived yet," says springheel, evassivly.

"i could go check at the store."

"look, they wont come in untill the relivent chit has been issued, vetted then counter signed."

"when will that be?" i ask as friendly as you like.

"why must you always come to me with problems rather than solutions, claudius? go and ask one of the brickys for a spair chisel, or something."

springheel realy can be quite blank and officious when the mood gets hold of him.

*   *   *

i back out the cabin, cut across to the caboos and just catch the last of the brickys as they head out onto site.

theres one fellow i recognise whos a bit friendlier than the others. he wears a waxed mustache and ive heard them address him as max.

i walk up to max just as his getting onto his motor assisted bike and ask if he has an old hammer and chisel i can borrow.

"just to get me by till bill gets
better."

    max pats himself down and feels in
his pockets.

    "no, not on me, son."

    i smile so's he knows i appricate
his performance. "is there anyone else
you can think of then?"

    "yes, as a matter of fact there is.
you go see jack nastyface over at the
ropery and tell him max sent you. he's
got tools coming out his bluddy ears.
if that shite hawk hasn't got it, then
nobody's got it. thats rite, isn't it
birt?"

    birt, pulls his bike up abreast of
max.

    "you sending the poor fucker to see
bob bishop?"

    max nods. "over the ropery, thats
where youll find the skiving barstard!
you cant miss it, its a bleeding mile
long. shite hawk be the 3rd man you see
sitting on his arse twiddlig his thumbs!
and mind he dont get you playing chess or
your'll have barnicals growing up your
legs!"

    i start walking.

    "you want to borrow anything, youed
best let nastyface win," shouts the one
called birt, "you no what they say, a

black dog for a monkey!"

i nod and smile. i dont know what on earth he's talking about.

"your bound to get lost. if your not back by nite fall we'll send out a search party!"

        ※   ※   ※

actually, its not very hard to find at all.

theyer not kidding either, the ropery disappears off into the distence, shrouded in mist. the cobbels come towards you, glisting in the rain, but far off the building is just a blur thru the drizzel.

i look in thru the gantry and ask a few smokers stood there where i can find this jack nastyface. 1st off they hide their snouts as theres a no smoking rule in there. then they see im just a sprog and start puffing away again.

"shite hawk? his nestled down in his box shed, just over yonder."

they nod towards some double doors.

the doors are wide open and you can see coils of rotting rope spiriling up to the cealing.

        i put my nose inside and call out
hello. theres an answer from somewhere up
the back. i pick my way thru the narrow
iles of coiled ropes. the whole place
is like a giant maize. i call out again
and he answers this time quite close by,
then i go around a blind corner and come
across a small little fellow sat there
dunking rope ends in a barrel of boiling
pitch.

        i tell him that the one called max
sent me.

        "max? i dont know no max. who's max
when he's at home?"

        "he's a bricky. he's got black hair
and a waxed mustashe."

        bob bishop looks distinkly
unimpressed.

        "he said you new him."

        all the while this jack nastyface
is picking apart the end of an old rope
that last saw action at the battle of
trafalga.

        "mister cubbit is off sick and his
tools are locked up in his locker and i
haven't got a key."

        nastyface nods to himself
thrortfully and dunks the end of the rope
into a cauldron of boiling tar.

        "mister who?"

"cubitt."

"what about your own tools? youre an apprentice aint you, didn't they give you a lovely set of brand-new gleaming chissels?" he asks selashiously.

"they haven't got them in yet. they'er waighting for a chit."

"waighting for a chit? bollox are they. listen, son your'll be waighting till doomsday. what are you, a bricky? and what would you be wanting with a mallet and chisels, anyways?"

"im a stonemason," i explain.

"stonemason!" bob bishop lets out a low whistle, "now theres a word i haven't heard spoken in donk's. who did you say your apprenticed to?"

"bill cubitt."

"cubitt? i know him. lives down my street. so thats what the old barstard does. i went to skool with him, or his brother. year above me he was. anyway, your waisting your time, he wont be teaching you nothing."

"why not?"

"why not? because he's had a bleeding heart attack, thats why not."

"really?"

"yes, really. or at least a stroke

173

or something."

"so he might be alright then?"

"who knows," says nastyface, "lets
just say they'ed neednt bury him just
yet, but they may as well not put the
spade back in the garden shed either."

nastyface licks his fingers and
tests the end of the rope to see if the
tars cooled then puts it to his tounge.

"who will teach me if he dosnt come
back?"

nastyface cocks his head and stairs
at me. "dont fucking ask me, im not your
fucking keeper am i? but there aint no
more masons, i tell you that much. and
your 'mister' cubitts too bissy snotting
up blud to teach a snot-nose like you!"
and nastyface smiles, pleased with
himself for managing to fit the word
'snot' twise into the same sentence.

nose bleeds? i'd seen those for
myself, that much is true. i can vouch
for this bob bishop's verasity there . . .

nastyface slings down the roap,
picks up another lose end and dunks it
into the smoking pitch.

"anyway, im stuck and was hoping you
mite see yourself the way to lend me a
few chissels and a mallet."

"were you, now."

"yes, max said you have everything in your junk shed."

"is that rite."

"yes, he said if you cant find it anywhere else, jack nastyface will have squirreld it away in his junk yard."

"he called me that?"

"yes."

bob bishop looks at me suspiciously. "what did you say your name was, boy?"

i look him straight back into my reflection in his specticals.

"i didn't say it was anything, but im called gustov."

"do you play chess, gustov?"

"yes, i can play chess." i answer rather haughtily.

"then sit down, and play." with one movement nastyface slings down the end of rope, pulls an old card table from benith the spinning jenny and emptys out a box of overly ugly, hand carved chessmen. the card tables painted with a chicky-chacked top.

"come on, sit down if you wannt to play."

bob bishop scoops up 2 pawns, juggles them behind his back then holds

them out front, perfectly hidden in his
tar'y mitts. i tap his left hand and he
shows me.

"white! your move."

and he spins the table round so the
white pices are on my side. i look at the
row of ugly chessmen stairing up at me.
some of the grimices on their kissers are
straight out of a horror show.

bob bishops face looms over the top
of them, his toung flicking at his lips
in anticipation.

"whats all that about, gustov?"

"what?"

"i thought you said you could play,
its your move."

i reach out and thoughtfully i move
my kings knight pawn 2 spaces. bob bishop
sits back and stairs at me, dumbfounded.

"you've moved knight pawn!"

i look at the pawn ceafully. yes,
its deffintly a pawn - though its been
carved with the head of a gudgion.

"i hope your not going to play all
irregular, gustov."

"how do you mean?"

"i mean all wierd and fucking
irregular. like that lad from the

boilermakers. he comes in here last
week, on thursday, all full of himself.
say's he knows how to play chess, say's
he learned it at some after skool club.
fine i say, sit yourself down, quoth a
brew and show us your best move. and he
sits rite in the exact same spot as you
are now and starts playing all higgle-
de-piggilldy. every move was a fucking
dissarster, back to front and inside
out. in the end i chucks my king down
and refuse to play the cunt. whats the
fucking point, because no one can play
someone who dosnt know not to play
higgle-de-piggilldy."

i nod. theres a long silence. it
soon becomes apparent that this silence
is never going to end unless i change my
opening move.

"whats rong with playing my king
knights pawn?"

bob bishop dosnt deam to answer me,
and turns his face away. after another
minite or so i lean forward, pick up my
knights pawn, replace it and move my king
pawn 1 space instead.

"dont move it co's i tell you to
move it!" barks nastyface.

i reach over and ruturn the pawns to
their originl positions.

"you need to make your mind up,
sonny jim!"

i look at him, but it really is
difficult to maintain eye contact.
suddenly he shouts at me.

"what's the point in the fucking
game if you do what your opponent tells
you? i may as well play my fucking self!
you've got to think for yourself, sonny
jim. your not going to get very far in
this fucking world if you cant think for
yourself, are you."

"i supose not," i answer
hesitatingly.

nastyface sits there glearing with
his hands on his knees.

"besides theres the touch rule: you
touch it - you fucking move it; you take
your hand off - thats it: move over, end
of story!"

i dont see much point in telling him
i know that already and only put it back
because his a big, cheating, swearing
baby.

"if you are going to move that
pawn move it 2 spaces not 1. whats the
point of crawling about the board like a
one legged cockroach? now come on, lets
start over again. and this time think!"

i pick up the kings pawn and move it
2 spaces.

"thats better! thats more of your
classic opening. which i will now counter

with my own kings pawn."

i move my kings bishop pawn.

"yes, the classic kings gambit,
which you will now see i respectfully
decline."

bob bishop moves he's queens knight
and i move my kings knight.

"for fucks sake!" nastyface sits
bolt upright, "no, no, no! wheres the
fucking sence in that? you've got to
think and move in pattens! or theres just
no point in playing at all!"

bob bishop makes as if to stand up,
so i quickly replace my kings knight and
move my queens nite instead. he looks
back at the board, and scratches his
narrow chin.

"ah, queens night to queen 3.
interesting move." he says, mussing to
himself.

it carrys on like this for the
next 20 minits. every time i make a move
i have to check nastyfaces face to see
if he approves of it or not. mostly he
contradicts me, then repremands me for
doing his bidding, and all the while he's
gleefully pilling up my pices along the
sink next to his elbow.

if i want to borrow a chisel, id
better let this nastyface win. with this
in mind i let him set up a honey trap

then send my queen blindly in.

"oh, i dont think you wanted to move there. look at this!" and he swoops on the board and whisks my queen away like some kind of chess vuture and sits back glowing with happyness at his magnificent victory.

nastyface comes round the table and claps me on the shoulder. "good game, sonny jim. i tell you what, that idiot from the boiler makers could lern a thing or 2 from you. says he plays chess but he dosn't know one squair from the fucking next. he played curry peter the other day - you know, the coloured fellow with the turban - the boy won of course, because he was so irregular, and curry peters good, bludy good. so anyway, i say's to him, the boiler makers apprentice, i say's 'i aint playing chess with you, you ackward little cunt, you can fuck rite off, co's ile not play chess with a cheat. and you can forget abot borrowing that asseterlin weilder as well!' . . . check mate!"

i look at the board. yes, its true. i smile at him weakly.

"get out of that if you can! you cant! boxed-in and buggered! another game?" he asks hopfully, and scoops up 2 pawns, and juggles them behind his back befor presenting he's fists to me.

2 hours latter i finnaly leave with 2 blunt chissels and a wormy old mallet.

i just make out the door when the cannon
goes off.

        *   *   *

next morning theres a note for me to go
over to springheels cabin. the upshot
is he sends me out labouring with the
brickies, which tekniqckly he's not
allowed to do. its a threat: the brickys
will down tools and refuse to sail. an
apprentice stonemason laying brick? it
would set a dangerous precedent. and
what about the insurance angle? im in
full agreement. you only have to have
half a brain to see the consequences, to
understand the further ramifications, the
subtler nuances.

i grab my sarnies and jump on the
ferry for hooness. i have to turn up my
collar and keep my cap pulled down so's
there chief sherang dosnt cop me. i hide
up the back amongst a bunch of aprentices
but just before we set sail im rumbeled
when they do a head count.

i stand on the steps and watch the
ferry set sail into the fog and moesy
back over to the cabin. i knock and
enter. old springheel survays me with
open disspleasure.

"so its you, back already?"

181

"yes," i answer.

springheel lets out a deep sigh. "you really like to be a problem, dont you, claudius? you refuse to fit in. why is that?"

i smile at him, which makes him look down.

"why couldn't you choose to become an electrician, or something usefull? something practical and easy to deal with? its as if you take a perverse pleasure in being akward and diffrent."

springheel flings his biro on the desk.

"you relise that we will have to send you to london to do your city and guilds, dont you? on block release! the other appretices can just walk up the road to the mid kent college on thursdays, but you have too choose to be a stonemason!" he shakes his head "do they teach stone masonry? of course they bludy dont! its a specialist course! well your one akward customer, claudius. why choose stonemasonry? theres just no sence in it!"

"i didn't really want to do stonemasonry in the 1st place. i wanted to go to art skool but i wasn't allowed," i explain, trying to calm him down.

springheel narrows his eyes and studdys my face cearfully.

"i like to think that the true adventurer goes forth aimless and uncalculated to greet unknown fate. dont you, mister brightstone."

"your telling me your not even interested in stonemasonry!"

i can see that springheel is getting pretty rieled up. "i wasn't at 1st, but now ive tried it i like it very much indeed." i add haistly.

"listen very cearfully, claudius, im not running around just for your amusment, theres plenty of other things i could be doing with my time, than fitting round your whims."

"yes, mister brightstone."

springheel scrapes his chair back and stands up.

"anyway, mister cubitt is on the mend, apparently! his wife say's that he will be in tomorrow."

"thats excellent news." i say with a little too much false jollyness. springheel checks my face for sarcasim.

". . . or if not tomorrow then monday . . . if his majisty feels up to it, of course."

"i could always go home . . . until he turns up, i mean . . . or i could go down to the dockside and make a drawing."

"very amusing. you will finish that cube your making. even if you have to carve it with your damn teeth. drawing on the dockside, indeed! now get out."

the whole street had a terrible and
windswept aspect. trees were quite bear,
scearsly a single leaf clinging to the
desolte twigs that flung and twitcht
against a gray sky. the autumn was over
and winter had gotten hold.

a scarlet bus sweeps past, the
conductor peering out the open back at
an old lady stood wrestling with a tartan
shopping basket on wheels. both the
ladys legs are bandaged up to the knee,
and above them a dusty blue coat flap't
about.

in a way, it seamed as if the very
wind hated her. she stars felornly after
the bus and the trees shake their twigs.
then the bus is gone and the old lady
also dissapears round the corner and i am
left quite alone.

5 minits previously a young man had
appeared from nowhere. over his shoulder
he carryid an old british army rucksack
and in his hand a canvas tool bag. upon
his head he wore a flat cap. if it was
not for an indigo blue cantonese jacket,
bearing a self embroided ying-yang symbol
on the breast pocket, you mite have
mistaken him for a plumber.

before the chance vanishes, i
should add that on the end of each leg
he sported an ancient boot. as he comes

nearer you can also see that under his
cantonese jacket he wears dusty overalls.

so this is our capitol. it seams
strange to be stood here seeing its
cheapness and ordinaryness. where are the
statues and glorius clock towers?

i walk down towards a main road
where there is at least an inkling of
another world: here you can actually
see buses and taxis criss-crossing
occasionally, and there are people
marching about, all be it not in scarlet
uniforms and bareskin hats.

a 100 yards on, just coming into
view, is my big brother, old nick,
walking with 7veral of his art skool
friends, singled out in a pair of navel
deck shoes, blanco'd white, and atop that
a donkey jacket featuring white plastic
shoulder protectors.

of course my hart swells with pride.
and why indeed wouldn't it? i am after
all his meek, younger brother. no matter
that all this dressing up is his attempt
at aluding to some vast expansivness of
mind, and is no doubt to be read as a
statement of independent thort, and the
fact that he is 'of our capitol' and has
removed himself from the provences and
the dominian of clod-hoppers.

the group moves benieth the limbs
of a great plain tree. they see me and i
wave but they do not wave back.

bitterly i relise that i have made
my 1st mistake. even if your wet behind
the ears you should know that you dont
go waving your arms about like some
imbercial at the 1st site of a pride of
lions.

the prospect of being near older
men must have excited my mind. to
further my delite, i see that they have
a butiful, ramshackle girl with them,
cear free and blond. prehaps i find all
of this 'newness' makes me imprudent.
yes, excitement is in my vains. when i
say 'older men', of course i mean art
students.

in futcher i must remember to hide
my open feelings.

here is a fact: my big brother has
always indevered to keep me hidden from
his friends. in our childhood home my big
brother ruled and bullied. this behaviour
was not only tolerated but openly
encouraged by our parents. why? because i
am a cinderella. in that respect he knows
that despite all his best efforts to
subdue me i will outshine him. so i must
be locked bellow decks.

but out here in the fresh 1 -
streets those old rules of power are
rendered inane and useless. of course
silence, and the walls of our home,
protected him. where as now, in this cold
air, i am free of his dumb tyranny and
his new found friends will see him with

all his glearing wounds and imperfections
illuminated.

yes, i feel that there will be many
opertunitys to humilate him.

they are walking straight towards
me and i am now able to decern particular
details: the shape of a nose, or the
pucker of the lips. my big brother
staggers, hands in pockets, mouth agape,
as if he is inebreated, or has been
smoking weed. is this his normal manner
or has he become affected? i am a werker
and they are the elite. also, i now see
that they in fact have 2 girls with them,
which is doubly exciting.

i for one do not drink nor smoke
drugs. to be presise i gave up alcohol
when i was 14, and thou i once smoked
weed as a 12 year old i have since ruled
such behaviour in myself unaccseptable.

we meet on a small patch of damp
pavement. my big brother is arrogant
and off-hand, bearly greeting me, only
managing to loudly obseve that i have
achny.

"this spotty specimen is my little
brother," he announces.

whilst he is at his most drugged and
bombastic i will strike, showing off of
my observational skills and damning wit.

is it rong to speak in such a way
about ones elder brother and superior? we

all head off as a group towards the squat
in c - farm.

＊   ＊   ＊

as we walk in that gathering dusk street
lites flickrt and start to come on. from
street to street the houses become more
dilapidated and blurred looking and the
pavement benith our feet more busted and
rubbish strewn.

        on either side whole terrices have
been ear marke't for demolition and have
corrugated iron banged up over the doors
and lower windows.

        not all of the street lites turn on
as many have had the glass smashed out of
them.

        we turn onto a little side street
and theres our house, the building they
squat. they occupy the ground floor and
the upstairs but the junkies have the
basement. apparently you have to go down
there to wash and get water but otherwise
it is important to keep the cellar door
baracaded. theres no tap or sink, just a
broken pipe hanging out the wall pouring
day and nite directly down a gurgling
black hole into the open sewer.

        the front railings have been ripped
of and you have to insert your hand thru

a gap in the corrugated iron to open the
front door.

the upstairs of the squat is
adoquet.

i follow them up the wooden stairs,
our feet banging on the bear boards, and
enter the upstairs front room. an old
thread-bear marrocan carpet has been
tacked to the wall in an artistic manner.
also a werking plug socet is located here
and an electric fan heater. the upturned
crate in the center of the room, around
which is arranged a verity of rotting
furniture, serves as a coffee table.

it is true that large arears of
plaster are missing from the walls and
the cealing rose has been stolen. also,
the windows have been boarded over and
the gaps stuffed with newspapers and
cardboard, and all of this is taped
together in a curious mosaic.

black mushrooms are in full bloom
benith the damp sills.

no, my new lodgins are not quite
as plush as my bedroom back home, but is
this a reason for a guest to brand the
hospitality squallid, or even turn his
nose up and refuse to enter such a rat
infested dump?

in all honesty my childhood bedroom,
which i still occupy, is itself damp
and freezing. you could even say that i
have grown accustomed or been trained,

if you will, for the sparten life of a
l - squatter. as much as i crave warmth
and snugness, it seams that it is not
nessisarly possible to set sail in life
and always expect flocks of roasted
pidgions to fly into ones open mouth.

there is no food so we have to
go and get chips. then they all want
to drink as well, so we jump the tube
barriers and ride to w - street and so
down to the union bar.

the place is quite jammed up and
full of ciggeret smoke. most of the faces
are talking between mighty puffs and
swiggings.

they all order dark pints. of
course i haven't drunk alcohol since i
was 14 and i have a small dry ginger ale
instead. i take out my pencil and draw
them as they tip their glassess.

there is a juke box playing in the
corner and a curious song starts up. i
put down my pencil. the voice is like
that of an old tramp crooning along
too an orchastra of buzz-saws and power
hammers. i ask old nick who it is but he
is too bissy gassing: apparently, if your
signing on at the dole office and run
into a group of gypsys, its best to tell
them that their children are beutifull,
they will then treat you as a brother,
rather than punch your lites out.

"one dosn't need to be afraid. just
look them in the eyes and complement them

on their children. it really is quite
exteroudenary. butiful children, really
quite tremendiously beautiful!"

it is suficeant to say that what
ever happens within auspice of old
nick's head is of monumental importence,
purly by virtue of being observed and
illuminated by his gagantuan brain. what
any other mortal would step over as cod-
roe is scrapped up and served up as
caviar on a gold platter: this much he
has lerned from our father.

i touch my big brothers elbow to
gain his attention.

"what now?"

"this song, do you know who its by?"

old nick cocks his ear. "no, but
its rubbish!" he turns his shoulder and
carrys on gassing.

im quite accustomed to my big
brothers unkindness and mildly carry on
sipping at my ginger-ale, thou of course
violently hating him from within.

to disipher the entire meaning of
the tune over the general din is not an
option but the whole effect is one of
anger, which matches my mood perfictly.
the song smashes its way towards its
climax of derision and power-hamers.
theres then a short pause before the next
record starts up: sacrin, insipid and
lacking in hatred. the long haires nod

there heads along to the beat and my big
brother carrys on exponding on the marvel
of 'the common touch', all the while
scowling his face as if in pain.

at this moment it really is possible
to see the damage done to my brothers
counternece by the harsh disinterest of
our absent father.

"look," my big brother suddenly
exclaims, jabbing his finger at a notice
board. his lips purse together and his
neck puffs up with blud, "why do you
think that person choose to pin that
poster in the top left corner of that
notice board?"

the others all mornfully turn their
heads and stair off into the smoked
filled room. yes, there really is a green
baize cloth board hung there, next to the
bar and there is the poster pinned in the
top left hand corner.

"you see - there it is, pure
abstract compersistion! why not put it in
the middle? or even in the bottom left
hand corner. why did he, or she, make
that particular decision?"

old nick swigs at his dark beer and
allows a supercilious smerk to form on
his wet lips, thoughly pleased with his
fantastic observational anallisiss.

it requires some effort to look
proudly on my big brother at this moment.
yes, he has certainly changed his tune

since having his cearfully exicuded
pencil drawing of a boot re-arranged
by the brush marks of john hoyland.
now it seams that drawing is dead and
life is pure brutality and 'abstract
compersition'.

no one has any more coppers left for
beer so its time to clear out, jump the
tube back to c - f - and weave our way
thru the barren streets.

i walk with these drunk ones to my
new home.

in the upstairs room drug ciggerets
are rolled and the girl with the blond
hair makes tea.

theres some quite appaling shadows
thrown up the walls and cealing by
those guttering candels. the fonds of
an old dying spider plant makes a fat
ceasars head, with hanging jowls and a
laurel riyith crown, and then a hoard of
hoplites turn up and shake their spears
at him.

after much talk and cearfull
ajustmets they lite up their trumpit and
pass it around. each in turn grasps the
cigeret between their ring finger and
pinky, then holding their fist to their
mouth and suck on it like a pipe. when it
comes round to me i decline my rite to a
puff and it passes on to the person sat
next to me.

i have my own special gingsing tea,

which i sip from a tin mug, and stick my
hand in my scran bag, which is tucked
out of site between my feet, and eat my
macrobiotic dinner: a handful of uncooked
brown rice and some grapes.

"you see where that window has been
boarded up?"

yes, it is my big brother, old
nick, again. he leans his large head back
and points. we all have to look to the
boarded up widow.

"there, on the left? why do you
think the person who plugged those gaps
chose to use the gray card at the top,
then the brown carton at the bottom? and
look, they have taped a cornflakes box
there but left lettering vissable on this
side."

one called ben, who is spouting
a scrappy black beard opions that the
fellow didnt like the draft and was
obviously making do with the the 1st thing
that came to hand.

"no!" shouts my big brother, "dont
you see, its all choices. choices of
placement. why do we make those desions?
as artists we all need to ask ourselves
these questions."

i squint at my scetch book and
stiffel a yawn. in truth im quite tired
and ready for bed.

"obviously they were just trying

to stop the draft!" reiterates one with
a pockmarked face and a very big plum in
his gob.

old nick shakes his head
sorrowfully, "but they still made a
choice. its still compersition. at a
fundemental leavel everthing is art!"

i try to swallow a few stubbon
grains of rice then swig them back with
tea.

"why dont people just paint
some good decent post impressionist
paintings?" i venture.

my big brother turns his bulging
eyes on me.

"because there fucking boring!" he
retorts.

*   *   *

gradually, as the smoke thickens, the
faces become more distorted and their
speech indistinct and slurred with
every puff. they make ever stranger
observations, which i actually find quite
elimentary, and eventualy very silly. it
seams that the more drugs they smoke, the
more like me they become. (till they tell
me that i must be high on their stinking
weed).

when i say that they become 'more
like me', of course they dont become
anything like me, but they still, never-
the-less, seam less puffed up and pleased
with their educated brains. except my big
brother of course, who remains thick-
necked and bombmbasic, despite sucking
down huge lungfulls of green smoke.

again the image of wooden puppet-
heads swirling in mist comes to mind.

is it really that i am a race
apart? or at least have one boot in the
gutter, whilest my fore head grazes the
angels? and peering from that place it
is sometimes hard for me to belive that
my fellow creatures are actually made
of flesh and blud, or even have beating
harts hidden inside them at all.

next to my tin mug is a cup full
of mould which has stuck to the cover of
a magazine lying on the upturned crate.
i have to pry it off cearfully to avoid
ripping the picture that lies undernieth,
and has been coily smiling up at me.
once i free the cup i lift the magazine
and peer at it. there is a girl pictured
there with her toung out dribbling
seamen from the corners of her mouth.

it is difficult for my hart and mind
to prossess the strange sensations. i
have to peer very closely on account of
the gloom.

in shock i replace the magazine onto
the crate.

how did such a girl come to be
photographed so?

"see, he's looking at that
magazine!" proclaimes my big brother.
i reach forward and turn the magazine
face down. "but he wont be getting any
girlfriends, not with that acny!"

the girl with blond hair looks
across to me and tenderly comes to my
deffence "i have more spots than him. i
just cover them up, thats all."

"but your beutifull, cleao," simpers
old nick, "where as that little shit was
born ugly!" and he makes a face at me.

when christ walked the earth
and said for us to become like little
children, could it be that he was trying
to remind us of gods presence in all and
aknowllege our devinty hidden benith the
barnical crust of our aquired karma and
to have trust in the universe and not
live life like fearfull, old hags wishing
ill on others? for certain, i doubt he
ment we were to smoke strong ciggarets
and revert to behaving like infantile
adults. as to buti, in essence, a child
dosnt judge, as it is still half in the
world of spirit, and is indeed a clear
lump of god. its fears and preferences,
thou seeded, have not yet begun to sprout
or burst forth into misserlyness and
depravity.

my big brother gets bissy rolling
another ciggeret.

so what if i have viewed a picture
of a woman dribbling cum from her lips?
what if i was allowed all 3 pleasurs and
too indulge in any depravity that took
my fancy? to command a legion of such
sluttish women? surly my hart and soul
would be burned out and all such futile
attempts to touch god, taste like ashes.
isn't it precisely because i have been
denied love, touch and intermacy that
i desire such things and have turned
everything into masterbation, and so
am to be punished yet again merely for
looking?

to destract myself i pass judgment
on the artistic placement of the rug,
which hangs, partially concealing
the gapping cavity of the ripped out
fireplace. i chomp on my lower lip, raise
my big toes inside my boots and stair at
the paterns thru the flickering gloom.

     *   *   *

it is not only my elder brother who can
fling acid about. no, being my fathers 2nd
son it is not against my nature to talk
in a desmisive and sarcastic fashion.
and in truth, lacking his education has
made me quicker witted than he will ever
be, only he's skill at crowing like a
parrot escapes me, but being born of his
desperation for our fathers love, it is
something i have scorned.

as we sit there in that desolate
front room, the eddies of pot smoke
entwining round our heads and shoulders,
it is me who emerges triumphant and
sober. indeed, everyone laughs at my
clever obsevations and is amazed that
i am far more surreal than they are,
without taking so much as a single puff
of their musty old ciggeret.

because hes assembled friends
laugh at my wit, my big brother too has
to pretend to find the whole situation
highly amusing, but all the while his
envious eyes rove from face to face
checking for love. at one moment he
grimices at me hostilely, the next he
smiles worridly.

that he would preffer me not to be
here in the world is obvious.

one wonders how the girl with blond
hair, who they call cleao, feels about
the picture of the girl dribbling cum on
the cover of the magazine. no one asks
her and if she is at all troubled by the
photograph she dosent show it.

thou she came to my defence
readly, she dosnt look at me or laugh
at my expert dissmissel of the artistic
placement of their pathetic rug. no, she
adds nothing new to the conversation.
all you can truthfully say about her is
that she is beautiful and silent.

i wish that i could one day talk too
such a woman.

tommorow i must rise early and
travel on the underground netwerk to s -.

         ✻   ✻   ✻

my bedroom is the downstairs front
room. theres no electricity so its not
possible to see anything. i unroll my
sleeping bag on an old army camp bed by
the lite of a candel, on account of the
cold and vicious damp i slide in fully
clothed.

        morning.

        i wriggle out of my sleeping bag and
stand shivveing in the gray lite. there
is no noise in the house and my breath
shows up like real fog.

        i go out into the hallway, take down
the baracade of old chairs and decend
into the cellar to brush my teeth. as
i decend into the gloom there is the
sound of running water and the laboured
breathing of a junky coming from the
black mouth of the coal-hole.

         ✻   ✻   ✻

outside the wind has dropped, theres
clear blue skys and glinting frost on the

tarmac. its not crawling with activity as no one exactly werks round here. i do see a postman but he keeps rite on going with his nose thrust in the air and dosnt deliver a single letter.

i trace my way back down to the tube station. along the way there is time to admire the last yellow leaf fall twise from the same tree. i watch as it drifts thru the air and hits the deck. quickly, i look up and there it is again awaiting its 2nd turn to fall from the fathermost twig of the plain tree.

whereas the leafs littering the street and gutters are trodden, broken and finished, this one is a real golden buti, more like an exsotic easten butterfly than a leaf. i waight for it to fall, but it decides to cling on, and it is still stubbonly hanging there as i turn the corner and loose site of it forever.

naturally i dont jump the barrier and go instead to the window where i buy a lergitamet ticket for my journy. theres a lot more people about now and i have to fight for my place on the lift.

within minits there are so many bodies crowding the platform that it is impossible to get onto the 1st train, which itself is already bursting at the seams as it pulls into the platform.

yes, theres a lot of shoving and we are so pushed up against one another

that in someways i would like to stop the
world and move amongst them as a ghost,
only pausing now and again to make love
to this or that beautiful women, before
moving on and pushing in at the front of
the que.

another train arrives 10 minits
later. considering the expence of
perchassing a little yellow ticket not
everyone gets a seat. surly someone
in a hat and wearing the appopreate
shinny buttons in a bright row of
authority could knock some sence into
this heaving crowed; or at least inform
the appropriate athoritys so as some
provision could be made to asure that
each and every paying customer enjoyed
the luxsory of a hard, unwashed seat.

the college is a suppriszingly
long tube ride down south. i could, on
reflection, have stayed at home and
come up to 1 - on the mainline every
day. an ingrate mite perhaps complaine
that the squat is in the rong district
altogether and imagin making loud
comments and demands of his elder brother
to re-locate. other mite put the blame
squarly on the shoulders of the college
or perhaps accuse the town planers of
negligence.

who ever it is that is a fault,
never-the-less it is quite simple
to negoshiate the route as all the
underground lines are colour coded for
ease of use and all a bumkin has to do

is get on board and stay on the black
coloured line all the way to s -. but it
isn't a 5 minit journy by any streatch of
the imagination.

and i assure you it is not possible
to travel among so many early morning
faces without at least peeping at some of
these sour mugs from out of the tail of
your eye. can all of these people really
be alive; to have had a childhood and
been babys and have bonafide memorys?
and then you start to wounding if there
is a soul in there at all. you are
either forced to become a christian and
try to love them all, or feel inclined
to join hands with the devil and stamp
on their heels and toes, cursing them
for cluttering up the world with their
bad breath, bow legs and size 13 feet.
honestly, to kick them all away like they
were a row of wooden skittles would bring
some supream satiisfation.

is it any wounder that sarcasim
has found its way into my mind? but my
mothers pridiction that i would never be
able to catch a train or find my way in
the world because of my backwardness have
proven false.

nor have i yet found myself getting
homesick for skool, as proffosized, and
my 'rude awakening' is evidently hidden
round some distant corner of the futcher,
licking its chops and grining with my
fathers face.

onece you fight your way out of
the tube station and disentagle yourself
from the heaving throng it is possible to
stand close by a lamp post and establish
your bearings.

so i find myself on a major road
- thrust up against some galvernized
railings - chock full of grinding lorrys
and red buses.

the building college is not so
difficult to spot, and i practice reading
its name. and even if you cant read, some
signs are perficly understandable, based
purly on the colour and scale of the
letters.

besides, if you cant read surly it
is still possible to ask!

a man selling newspapers studies
my face with open disdain and points his
finger up at the building oppersite.
yes, the name is ritten there, emblasend
across its top in 3 ft high letters.

i cross thru the crawling traffic
and enter thru the main doors. there i
ask the doorman where i can find the
stonemasons depatment, which he tells me
is across a courtyard out back.

thinking about it - using pictures
in my mind - that newspaper sellers hand
really was like a bundle of dry sticks
with one particularly knobbly knuckle
thrusting away, almost jabing the roof
off the building in its urgency to spell

out the letters for me. also he had an
unpleasant tendency to bark in my face,
as if i was deaf and dumb, as well as
blind.

the building is of concreat.

*   *   *

the other apprentices are not shy and
reticent in the least. theres plenty of
swearing as they lean at their respective
benches, thumbs hooked in their belts
chewing gum and scowling at me as i
enter.

i look about that dusty werkshop.

yes, im the new boy.

rite off there are some impolite
comments made about my cantonese jacket
with my self embroided ying-yang on the
breast pocket. and all the while our
tutor just stands their in his brown
werk coat, smiling along in compleat
agreement. he has dark hair and looks for
all the world like a greengrocer with a
real turnip for a nose.

all the other students seam to know
each other.

actually there is good reason why
i wear my cantonese jacket. not only
dose it differentuate me from the avarge

student by pointing to other experences
and interests outside of chipping stone,
but whilest in 1 - i will be practising
tia chi at the central practice skool
with the proffesor.

a fellow on the next bench, 7veral
years older than myself, is also stood
alone. this one wears a beared, smokes
a pipe and smiles 3 or 4 stained and
sharpened teeth at me. from these signels
alone it is possible to decern he's
sensitivity and overall seperetness from
the gang.

his name is richard.

is it strange, or in anyway
unnatural, that i should gravitate
towards him and he likewise to me? of
course not.

our 2 benches are over to the rite,
just as you enter the room.

i smile and nod to richard and im
just going to start up a little chat when
the tutor calls me out front, hands me a
pile of illegible gastenered papers and
tells me to go round the class handing
them out to each student. we all have to
read these forms then sign them in blue
or black ink then hand them back in. next
we troop out to the yard and collect a
lump of stone off the tecknition, whos
stood there smoking a ciggeret with his
foot up on a lump of rock, then its tea
break.

we file out of the room, me and
richard going last.

there is another student within
our midst, hidden out back in the
greengrocers office, where he is
apparently carving a materpice. the 1st we
see of him is when he shuffels into the
canteen with his eyes cast down. he has
dark eyebrows, a wide nose and a brown
forlock, giving him the apperence of a
sucking calf. this enterty is apparently
the greengrocers protojay.

thare no seats left where the other
apprentices sit so me and richard have
to find a table and sit on our own, for
which we are labelled as 'queers'. i buy
a banana and get some hot water for my
ginsing tea. really, one of the bolder
appretices calls out to me that i like
richard to stick his beardy chin up my
arse.

i have to pretend not to here him.
richard explains to me that where as all
the other apprentices come from a single
yard somewhere out west - that apparently
specializes in breeding course, idiotic
automatons - richard, like myself, is
a lone apprentice. he himself has been
forced to chip stone purely for the
satisfaction of some ancient uncle who
once owned a monumental masonry yard
and whos dying wish was to see his only
nephew suffer as he once suffered.

it is very interesting to watch

richard smoke his pipe, which he puffs
into life quite effortlessly. the main
thing you notice is the smell, which is
like an exotic bonfire. i too would smoke
a pipe and in fact fully intend to do
so, despite the derision i will incure
from the faint harted and paintently
unoriginal.

in this way we amuse ourselves
during the lunch break: where as the oafs
scoff baked beans and hessitatingly lite
cheap ciggerets, we obstaine from food
and create dense clouds to hide in.

richard re-fills his pipe and shows
me how to spark-up: the trick is not
just to puff away, liting match after
match, but to create some extra draw by
stickiing your thumb in the bowel and
getting a real draft going. also, blowing
air back thru the pipe gets the embers
raging. in short - you cant pussy foot
with a pipe and have to show the bryer
whos boss.

on the way back to class we spy
the special student again, this time
lurking in the corridor, quickly he is
ushered into the store cupboard by the
greengrocer. indeed he is a rare prize
and possesion.

tequcknickly we are not allowed to
sit on our benches and are required to
stand. the greengrocer comes out of the
store cupboard, and 7veral rough fellows
slide to the floor. the greengrocer gives

them a look, then makes sure the store
room is firmly closed behind him, before
walking to his desk.

there are only 8 pairs of tin-
snips between the lot of us and the
greengrocer directs us to pair up and cut
out templates, which we are then to use
to scribe a pattern onto the ends of our
stone blocks.

according to the greengrocer these
pattens must then be carved perfectly
true from one end of the stone to
t'other.

looking about me, at the industry
- stone chips flying about my ears, like
hot metiorites - im forced to ask myself
if im at all up to the task that life has
set before me and if indeed masonry is,
by its nature, mearly a craft reserved
for nit-picking imberceals, obsessed with
prosission and fractions.

(of course the author realises that
harmless chips of portland stone are
completely unlike metiorites or comets.)

as well as droaning at us, this
tutor of ours also illustrates his verble
insructions with painfully slow movements
of a crumbling pice of chalk acroos an
ancent black board.

i really try to listen to this
greengrocers droneing monotone, but it
is impossible for me to focus, or hear
anything much over the insessent taping

of chissels, clunking of falling stone
blocks and the screeching of the chalk
as it suddenly scurrys across the black
board and bangs out a full-stop.

whatever is the matter with me?
am i now to grand and important to
lower myself to learning? i am only 16
years old and bearly out of skool, is
it already impossible for me to study
as i once did? and whatever happened
to the cheerfull young lad with the
startling ability to memorise list after
list of facts, and dutifully follow the
instructions of my betters to the letter?

after making one pefict tomb stone
we'er supposedly equipt to carve out a
thousand more. we chip away all afternoon
fashioning our decorative geisons,
whilest our vegitable nosed tutor makes
the rounds, picking holes in our handywerk and occasionally offering up a rear
complement.

up and down the iles he goes,
nodding and smiling. to be truthfull,
he really only sings the praises of one
student in particular. one wonders if
this speciman too will shortly be whisked
away to the hallowed store cupboard,
there to be groomed for excellence by the
greengrocer.

our tutor props the block on
its side and draws attention to some
miraclious detail of perfection, which
to any seeing eyes is ham fisted and

average.

when the grocer comes level with
mine and richards benches, he makes
as if to pass us by, then drematickly
turns, comes back and commences to loudly
list and report our short falls, thus
illustrating to the other students what a
pair of dundder-heads we truly are.

"pick up your mallet, lad."

i do as he tells me, and he comes
round, stands behind me and takes charge
of my mallet hand and chisel.

stood there, with his chin on my
shoulder, i can see the bobble of his
turnip nose out of the tail of my eye,
and also smell his utterly disgusting
breath.

"now let this arm go lad. come on,
relax. your not trying to build your
byceps up now. your not mister universe,
are you?" and he looks round the room
for the laugh. "let the mallet do the
werk . . . have you ever held a claw
before? . . . really? you woundnt have
thort so. look, you need to tidy these
lose chippings off the bench, and from
the floor. its an accident waighting to
happen. one thing i will not tolerate in
my classroom is slothernly behaviour.
ask any of the lads. what is it i wont
tolerate, boys? thats rite, sluthenly
behavior! . . . oh, you can smoke at the
bench if you must, but i wont have drunks
in here wielding chisels. now cearfull.

have you ever studied gemomotry? i thort
not! what are you doing, boy! for christ
sake slow down. dont hack at it, your not
chopping grandmothers kindling, now. take
it easy. ile give you all the guidence
you need if your just let the mallet do
the werk. do you trust me? you think you
know better!"

in this way the greengrocer
encourages even the more timid of the
students to openly mock me.

※   ※   ※

its only at dinner time that i discover
that me and richard are the only 1st year
students on the course. all the others
apprentices are in the 2nd or even 3rd year
of their studdys. is it really fare to
measure our handy werk against someone
who has been chipping away for 3 whole
years?

※   ※   ※

richard stands with his pipe clentched
between his teeth, walloping the dainty
little chisels with a mallet the size of
a loaf of bread. when our esteamed tutor
rubukes richard for his lack of delicacy
- pointing to the irregularitys in his

handywerk - richard mearly removes his
pipe from his teeth and states quite
calmy that it is his belith that verity
is the very spice of life. our tutor
looks at him with crossed eyes.

for my part, i find it preffrable to
lay down my chisels and make some sketchs
of the others bissyly at werk.

im in the middle of drawing richard
liting up his pipe when he makes a signel
at me with his eyes. i turn to see old
turnip nose stearing at me. i put down my
sketch book and start examing my block
of stone. our tutor demands to see what
i was drawing and chuckels quitly to
himself as he flicks thru the pages.

"come with me." and he turns on his
heel and marhes off. i have to follow him
to his office. "come on, if your coming.
just in here. now ile show you some reall
art!"

we pass thru the 1st vestible and
then onwards into the innermost chamber.
where, once inside, i have to vew the
hatefull masterpice being created by his
'protojay' - these are the terms i use in
my mind, to make this 'chosen one' less.
yes, i even say 'chosen one' to myself
in a mocking way - his werk lies their
on a bench surrounded by dust and stone
debris.

what at 1st mite strike you as
remarkable is, in effect a poor relieaf
of a soldier dutifully copied from

a silver point by leanardo devinci. certenly some signifcent skill was required to emulate the exsessivly flamboyant style of the helmet, and im the 1st to admit that it didn't carve itself.

as i stand there with a grin of pain fixed on my face, the greengrocer pulls out a file of photograps, detailing the various stages of excelence the protojay has passed thru. i am even shown the minute files, some of them the size off meer toothpics, which the protojay uses to emulate the frills and scrolls that litter the head of this, frankly, girl-like warrior. yes, the protojay has somehow managed to rob the soldier of his mascunlinity and given him the pouting mouth of a skool girl.

personally speaking i find the finickity nature of the carving and overall ostentatious showing off of this 'protojay' vomit inducing. detail and perfection is one thing but even god dosnt fling it in your face to help him feel better about his obvious inadiqueses.

no, i will never be left in peace to make carvings of indian heads. i refuse to show off my skills i will always be labelled as ham-fisted. the terrible truth of stonemasonry is that its essential hart is mindless repitition. even if carving a one-off gargoil it seams that fractions and

elaborate scrolls of death are the order
of the day, where as i can only live by
verve and wit.

is that high blown of me: announcing
myself in such a way?

          *   *   *

on the homeward journy i follow a girl
down the tube station tunnels and touch
her.

of course, i didn't realise that
i was following her and rather than me
trailing her it was more of a case of her
following me from in front.

1st off i try to pass her in the
ticket hall, and if she had allowed me to
do so, that would have been an end to it.
of course i noticed her stood in front of
me, but was nether-the-less happy to give
her up and walk on.

why, instead of allowing me to hurry
past did this girl increase her pace, as
if purpossly keeping in front and make
it possible for me to ignore her sexual
buttocks, displayed with a deep split.

just in this way i am drawn to her
and quicken my pace to keep up.

suddenly my path is blocked by the
legs and unbrallers of 7veral busness

men, who are apparently immune to her
charms and quite happy to clutter up the
tunnel and allow this sexual vision to
slip away unoticed. i am on the point of
loosing site of her, when she decides
to stop and bend over slightly, as it
were. of course, when i again summon up
my resolve and try to over take her she
simply gallops off. in short - she is
enticing me.

now the chase is on, i hurry to
catch up, but this time i am obstructed
by 2 female comutors disscussing
lipstick. when i finnaly battle my way
thru and arrive on the platform the girl
is no where to be seen.

i stand alone and crest fallen. i
check along the entire platform, but she
is lost. all the faces look quite dead
and i look up at the coloufull posters
thay have there, advertising all sorts of
irrelivent rubbish.

presently the train rolls in. i
postion myself where i belive the carrage
will stop and the doors open. i am about
to step on board when, from nowhere my
doe spings forth and pushes directly
in front of me, again dissplyaing her
buttocks. with no seats available, and so
little room to stand i am forced to press
in behind her. indeed she is inviting me
to touch her accdently.

it is quite hard to breath in that
atmaspher. it is as if i can here my

own hart beating over the juddering and swaying of that carrage. and all the while i have to try to concentrate to sink my chi, as instructed by rupurt, thus stopping myself be flung about by the sudden motions of the carridge.

the girl gets off at a stop befor mine and i can feel her commanding me to follow.

i jump off and keep 7veral paces behind her. assending the moving stairs, she stops and look back at me. she has the same lips as the girl dribbling cum, she tosses her head and look away. i step up and slowly allow the knuckle of the middle finger of my left hand to at 1ˢᵗ rest against her buttocks, then push into the split. my hart is thumping in my head. im going giddy again and once more can scearsly breath.

and now the wooden steeps are flattening out - as we reach the top of the moving stair case - to be sucked back benieth us. my mouth is dry as dust as we are forced to step off into the ticket hall. here i stagger and fall down as she disappears into the nite.

✳   ✳   ✳

of course this temptress has been touch't in a despicable manner by an unkown

stranger. and i state quite clearly that
this unknown stranger is myself, but in
my defence i am also unknown to myself.

i realise that this is no defence.

apart from the fact that we are all,
to a greater or lesser extent, despicable
strangers, and life is a big, indecent
game of tag, it is still rong to give
into base urges. besides, we perverts
dont just pass pain and torment on, we
keep a great big personal chunk of it for
ourselfs.

i am reffering to being systmaticly
fondled over subsequent nites by the fat,
hoary hand of a man when i was 9 years
old. thou to speak of such things is
indelicate, and i will not be induced to
do so.

i walk up the barren street to the
sqwat.

theres a stink back at the squat
because ellegiddly i didn't re-enstate
the barrier at the top of the cellar
correctly. a blow heater from upstairs is
missing, plus the long playing records
from our childhood, which my brother
brought with him to 1 -, are gone.

it seams that the junkys managed to
kick their way in and steal anything that
wasnt nailed down.

so to my camp bed, and i rite by
candel lite:

dear girl on the tube train, permit
me to undress you and rub my eyes all
over your body; to follow you and molest
you in my mind; to reduse you to a
harmless object. becouse i would never
truly love you. because i am a coward of
sex.

the students sat cross legged on the
bare boards. a cold draft was coming in
through a yawning gap under the main door
and aimed rite up my trouser legs.

at once the main door opens and
a small, gray, balding man enters the
brightly lit drill hall. the entire
asembly stands. the masters, stood at
our front, place their right fists into
their open left palms and bow deeply. we
novises follow suit. the professor, for
thats whos just glided in, returns our
bow.

another question, was the professor
actually hovering across the dirty wooden
floorboards without so much as touching
the ground? some would try to convince
themselves so. that the proffessor had
'certen powers' was widely put about,
but others would poo-poo the notion and
point to the fact that the professor
had 2 feet for a good reason. but there
was no argument as to the proffessors
attire: he was dressed head to foot in a
glowing white cantonease suit with black
trimings, and was bissyly wrinkling his
forehead and smiling his chinease eyes at
all and sundry.

the gift of my drawing to cyclops
has not made him my friend after all.
if i was expecting an heros welcome from
him, i was mistaken. it is true that

he dose nod at me, but one cant help
but feel that he is ashamed of my lowly
stature, espesherly when standing next to
his fellow students of a more advanced
level.

from my postion at the back it is
possible to decern what people describe
as 'an electricity in the air'. so this
is their famous proffesor drifting about
as lite footed as a kitten. you really
are forced to look up into the dim
ressess of the rafters to see if there
isn't a puppet master balancing up there,
pulling on his strings.

over by the door sits my big
brother, old nick with 2 of his student
friends. they have come along to wittness
this proffesor chee soo with their own
eyes. yes, old nick follows me as if it
is me who is the elder brother and he the
younger, thou of course the oppersite is
true.

lined up against the wall in our
yellow jackets we must look for all the
world like a row of cannerys on a wire.
which makes our black jacketed masters
crows over a corn field.

chee soo takes his ritefull postion
at the front of the class and studies
our faces cearfully. there is absolute
silence. finnaly his toung comes out and
licks at his gray coloured lips.

"i see new faces amongst us, as well
as many old friends. all are welcome."

222

there follows a long pause as the
professor considers his next sentence.

stood there, with eyes closed, who
knows if peace rains in his mind or if he
isnt just going thru the motions.

"all people visit this earth plain
many times. sometimes a soul will return
as human, sometimes as an animal. if they
have lead a bad life, maybe they will
return as a pig, or a dog."

he scans us all meaningfully.

"no one here, i take it, wishes
to return as a pig?" we all glance at
each other then look back to chee soo.
his face is taught and serious, but
also, a twinkle can be detected in his
small brown eyes. one of the masters
even attempts to laugh. chee soo nods in
aprovel, titters grow, then breake out
into overly hard and sharp laughter. chee
soo has made an ancient chinnese joke.
chee soo rises his hand and abruptly the
laughter ceases.

"now, every body stand with their
feet hip-width apart, in ridding horse
posture," and chee soo leads us, bending
his legs, knees slightly apart and his
hands at his hips, as if holding the
raignes of an imaginary horse. "open
the chest. allow the shoulders to relax.
increase the gap between your ears and
you shoulders. tuck the chin in. face
forward." and we mimick his look of
serious intent.

again the proffessor throws his gaze
around the room, allowing it to settle
here and there like a magnifying glass
burning up ants.

"the horseman, surveying horizon.
the horseman knows where he has travelled
and where he is heading. i was an ophan
boy and lost both my parents at a young
age. my father was chinease and my mother
english.

"i was brought up in a benardos home
in l -. one day, whilest playing in the
park, i kickt my football and it hit an
elderly gentleman who was sat on a bench.
i ran over to collect my football and
saw that he was a chinease man. before
the war there were very few chinease in
l -, so we got to talking and that was
the begining of a frendship that was to
change the direction of my life.

"that mans name was mister lee.
the lee family had been practicing the
ancent ways for generations. in those
days the teachings were only passed down
thru close family. but mister lee had
no son and as our frendship grew mister
lee decided to adopt me as his nephew
and start training me in accordance
with the way of the tao. who knows what
past life connection existed between us
to facilitate that 'chance' encounter
- if of course there is such a thing as
chance, which there isn't.

"as i look about the room today

i already recognise one person who i
sheared a past life with. i wont say who
it is, but they know who they are."

i would like to stand and look about
the room at the other faces but it is
quit unessisary as its obvious that the
proffesor is talking about me.

by now my knees are screaming to
come out of riding horse posture, but the
proffesor is completely oblivious to our
discomfort.

is it possible that i did some
heinous rong to this proffessor in
a past life? and will he be seeking
satisfaction? that he is angry is evident
from the way he arches his eyebrows and
turns his pupels into pinpricks.
at last we are told to stand and his gaze
moves on, penertrating walls and peoples
skulls along the way.

after warm-up we practice looking
at auras. 1st we have to focus on the edge
of the main entrance door frame, then we
move on to the sides of people heads.

"some of you will be able to detect
a faint glow. this is the field of energy
that surrounds all objects and entertys.
with practice you will be able to decern
an indevidules aura and their intent."

next we stand on one leg and rotate
our ankles whilest sinking our chee
bellow ground. in this way we make our
self double heavy and less prone to being

kicked aside.

to finish up chee soo takes us
thru some chee gong exersises. for
his fernarly, the proffessor stands at
one end of the hall, in ridding horse
posture, and summones the 3 masters - and
cyclops - to attack him in mock combat.

his attackers come stelthely,
sliding across the boards. they break
left and rite, encircling chee soo, who
now rises into stalk posture, whilest
flexing his eyeballs in concentration.
one after the other the masters, and
cyclops, attack from the 4 corners.

despite his tired, decrepid looking
face, the proffesor is quite spritely
and wirls amongst the dark muscular
forms like a dainty little top. why the
professor should be so much more agile
than men 1/2 his age is hard to nail
down, but is apparently the whole point
of his absurd practice.

it seams that god takes some chosen
ones and blesses them with a particular
unexpected talent that others - no matter
how dutifully they emulate and try to
pursue excellence - will never match.
yes, the proffessor side steps them all
and we watch in ore as they fall like
weeds, sythed into harmless little heeps.

it is not even possible to see
by what means they are knocked to the
ground. it is as if by will alone that
the proffesor courses them to trip over

each other and wriggle on their backs
like over turned beetles.

there they roll, boss eyed,
completely dissorentated. then, with a
shake of their groggy heads they spring
back up like sunmmer flowers, ready to
be mowed down afresh . . . they start,
stagger and stop, circling like hyenas
. . . one lunges in dragon posture. again
chee soo daintly side-steps then deftly
taps the fellow on the shoulder, sending
him crashing into the wall. another is
hurled, spawling towards the doorway. a
3rd, old cyclops, is stopped dead in his
tracks by a touch to his sola-plexus.
he gasps for air and drops to the floor
whimpering.

with this the professor places his
hands on his womenly hips and allows
himself a little smile of triumph.

in such a way it is possible to
decern the delite that this professor
takes in expressing his gifts in front of
an admiring audence.

yes, our famouse proffessor is truly
invinsable.

yet one couldnt help but be
suspicious that those big louts, who just
now had been so roundly humiliated and
made fools of by our tiny dervish were
not really trying their hardist.

surly it wouldnt be that difficult
for one of those young brutes to grasp

the old raskel round the neck and hold
him down till the others have the chance
to give him the beating he so richly
deserves. are they in his pay or could
it be that they are too shy of landing a
well armed blow and so knock the annoying
little manikin senceless?

how kind and unkind we are to
diffent people. some fellows we applaud
for being cut-throats, some we despise
for their meekness, by this measure we
can decern which apects of ourself we are
at home with and which we disdain.

at the end of the training session
a raffle is held and i win electronic
edition of the tao te king and my big
brother and his 2 friends sign up
to learn the way of the tao from the
professor.

the tea huts of hell

a cannon goes off.

out swarm the hidden werkers: from
the bowls of mothballed ships, springing
like cats to the quay side, they come.
trapdoors lift from duggouts and heads
emurge sleepy eyed from sheds and rusting
nissen huts.

still others desend like tattooed
monkeys from the lattice-werks of crains
that line the wharfs, hands skipping down
the ladder runs without even using their
tootsies. once they hit the deck theres
scearsly time for a scratch and a fart
before they tuck there necks in their
fearnaughts and its off for the gates.

bicycles clatter over the cobbels
- a street of babys heads a 1/2 mile
down the side of the ropery. a wheel
gets caught in the train rails . . .
someone swurves . . . the admriles staff
car bibs its horn. everyone has to get
home, rite this instant, heading for the
allotment and the boozer!

an ants nest has been kicked open.

this is the picture sketched in
by an expert hand. someone with a more
delicate stomach mite pause to vomit.

see the faces grown premitualy old, each
smashed face with a tidemark round its
neck, black as a hangman's noose, and
a whole nest of black-heads enjoying
themselfs round the nostrels.

outside the main gate the weather
is much the same: another heaving mass of
caps and elbows shoving to get onto the
last bus home.

next morning the moon drags them
out of bed and washes them back in for
breakfast and a snout. a great tied of
unwashed flesh.

thats how nanna lewis used to tease
granddad: 'they go to muster at 7.30 then
have a tea break: thats not werk, thats a
rest camp!'

thats not strickly true.

newspapers, tea mugs, toast
then theres scearsly time for a doze
before its time to down mugs and head
out onto site. often its cold out as
well, and wobbling over cobbels isn't
as comfortable as nestling down on fat
pillows and eiderdowns.

the cavalry sit, legs cocked at
the ready over bicycles. the poor bluddy
infantry go on foot, a stroll round the
block then dodge back indoors for a kip;
a safe cubby hole below decks. some
really have to pretend to werk.

it's a world apart in here, old lags

from the last war and some from the 1st,
then the national servis boys as well,
all sitting on high and judging students
and the unemployed. which ever way you
look at it its plain that the world is
lacksidaisical and full of skivers.

we troop off thru the drizzle.
bill wobbling from side to side, his fat
little legs making occassional pumping
movements on his boneshaker, then free
wheeling with a fag hanging from his gob.

i strike out on foot, all the while
avoiding being hit in the calf's by one
of bills pedels. i run on ahead and bill
shouts at me to slow down. i pull up and
let him catch me.

"what the f- are you trying to
prove? theres no sence rushing around
and getting your knickers in a twist!
springheel knows it takes us 20 minits to
get out onto site. at the rate your going
we'll be there in 5. think about it.
thats rite, its a dangerious president.
now walk on, but nice and slow mind."

once out on site we bung on the tea
fanny and dust the tools down, just in
case it stops raining and we can venture
outside. and of course springheel mite
show his sour mug.

after that its dinner time, and whos
got the spirit for werk after feeding
their face?

bill does his crossword puzzel and i

listen out for the 3.30 cannon.

theres only 15 minits till home
time when someone clocks springheel jack
walsing along the basin. an instentainous
hammering starts up a good hundred yards
ahead of him as each look-out cops a
ganda. and so the clattering procceds him
weather he goes in the yard, and like a
tiger hunting in the jungle, he looks up
and curses the monkeys that announce his
wearabouts to the world and his wife.

yes, whatever doorway springheel
pokes his nose in he finds hard werking,
industrious fellows, breaking their backs
for king and country.

bang - bang - bang! thats the
signel for us to look lively and start
brushing off some crumbs.

bill sets down his mug, puts the
biscits away in his donky box and lifts
out the masons mallet and starts show me
a few licks. its a pretty hefty, a lump
of beach wood, shaped like a loaf of
bread on a stick.

"will you ever listen, use the
waight of the mallet, for gawds sake! you
carry on like that yourll end up with
fore armes like f-ing pop-eye!"

i nod and start chipping away.
meanwhile brincat wonders in rubbing his
eyes and yawning.

"where the f- have you been?"

brincat shruggs his boney shouldrs.
"well dont just stand there. if
springheel walks in now he'll be pleased
as punch! go make yourself scearse . .
. i dont know where! . . . hide up the
back, pull the sale over your head or
something."

bill survays the room to make sure
eveythings ship shape and well hidden.
"f- mine, who left the f-ing sause bottle
out? . . . well stow it! and you, at
least look like your werking!" bill comes
over, snatches the mallet out my hand and
shows me the real way to do it. "put your
back into it! you've got to learn to look
bissy. no matter what, never let the
nobs see you relaxing yourself. if your
going for a stroll, pic something up and
carry it - it dosnt matter what it is -
an empty tin buckit does the job nicely,
but always, always have something in your
hands and look like your going somewhere
to do something very important. and dont
let them see you gawping up at the clouds
or catching blinking flys, they'll put
you on a fizzer. besides, what happens
when old springheel sees you sunning
yourself on my watch? it comes back to
me, dosnt it! think about it. so look
lively and shiver those blinking lumps of
rock!"

we all keep hard at it for 5 solid
minits but there no sign of springheel
jack, its a false alarm. we downs
tools, roll snouts and sit back on our
palliases.

i preffer to pull out my sketch
book and do some drawing. bill nips out
his roll up, covers his face with his
handkercheif and immediately starts to
dose. suddenly he snatches the hanky from
his face. "i tell you what, springheel
must have been called back to his cabin,
but you mark my words, the sods onto us.
his after you brincat, its only a matter
of time." then he goes back under his
hanky.

brincat saunters back in and slumps
against the door frame. i start drawing
his nose, its going pretty well but then
he feels my eyes on him and he scowls,
gets up and mooches off. i had his pointy
profile pretty well sketched in as well.

bill pulls the rag from his face,
"oi, brincat! why dont you sit still
for gustov. he's only drawing you, you
missrable bugger, he wont steel your
soul." bill winks at me, pleased with his
joke. "sod him, you can draw me instead."

i start to draw bill.

bill looks at me with a fixed smile.
"brincat! come over and see this! it mite
be worth millions when his famouse." bill
stands, comes round and looks over my
shoulder. "you like your art, dontcha,
boy? can i have it to show the misses?"

"im keeping them so's i can apply
to art college."

bill sucks his teeth. "nah, your

pulling my pisser! tell me your pulling
my pisser! art college? christ, theres no
money in that, boy!"

"but its what i want to do."

bill shakes his head and relites
his rolly. "nah, theres no security. its
a mugs game. do it in your spair time,
as hobby, maybe, but the dockyard's for
life. become a blinking student? they've
got soft hands!" bill grabs my sketch
book, "you give it to me. and make sure
you sign it!"

then the canon goes off - ka-boom!
it ecoes out across the estery. thats our
starting pistol. we'er off!

basicly we drop everything and
scarper. in 5 minits those funk holes are
like the mary coleste; hot cups of tea,
half eaten digestive biscits, a fag butt
still smouldering in an ashe tray: an old
backy tin nailed to the bench. but not
a man in site, just the dockyard moggy
stuffing his whiskers in a can of manky
condenced milk.

of course, brincats apparently
hidden away somewhere under the pyramid,
feeding tit-bits to furrycat, but only
bill knows where.

⁂

next morning its the same story: you bung
you card into the clocking-on machine, it
'tings', stamps the time and date, you
stuff it back into the brown card wallet
with your name typed on it and duck your
head into the tea huts of hell.

by and by i decide that i really
should bite the bullit and start smoking
a clay pipe. nothing modern or fancey,
real old skool jack-tar.

when i change buses on the way home
there is a newsagents with a fine display
in their front window. they have all
manner of pipes with different shapped
stems. the mouth pices of the clay pipes
have all been dipped in scarlet paint.

maybe ile choose the one with a
hawks head on the bowel, or perhaps
a scull and cross bones, or just the
profile of a salty sea-dog.

※   ※   ※

i get hot water for my ginsing tea, take
the pipe out of my bag, cearfully unwrape
it from its tissue paper and fill it with
balkan sobrani. then i strike a mtch and
give it a good suck.

theres quite a lot of coughing and
the clay mouth piece sticks to my lip.
everything werks fine with it, its just

a matter of not snatching it from your mouth and inadvertently ripping a lump of flesh with it. also, keeping it alite and not having the stem get backed up with stray crumbs of tobacco is a challange. plus the bowl heats up pretty sharpish and becomes tricky to hold. nor can you exactly clench the stem in your teeth as it is liable to snap off.

"you cant smoke that! you ant earned the respect!"

i look over and see brincat stood by the tea fanny.

"hello mate." i call back, and give him an insolent thumbs up.

"i aint your fucking mate!" he snarles back at me.

"have you seen bill?" i ask mildly.

"wouldn't tell you if i fucking had." shouts brincat, rite across the room.

i try to smile at him, but its impossible to look into his angry face.

there i sit and prod at my pipe. the tabbaco has formed into a hard, chard plug thats wedged into the bowl and wont come out. i try to dislodge it with a burnt match which instantly snaps in two.

an old fellow leans over and hands me his penknife. he has quite a scearry set of false gnashers that seam to be 2

sizes too big for his mouth. i thank him
and manage to get the bowl pretty cleaned
up. i hand the knife back and thank him
again.

not only is this fellow got a pair
of false teeth fit for a horse, but he
is also wearing a copper fleck't jacket,
cunningly tied at the waist with a bit
of old tar'd rope. deep within the dark
tweed it really is glittering with
flashes of gold and sparks of blue. i eye
the jacket enviously.

"i like your jacket."

"what this old thing? i wore it as
a boy. the mrs was going to throw it out.
no, i said, i can wear it to werk."

i nod and start re-packing my pipe.
im actually down to my last 3 matches.
thats nearly a hole box just to get it
going for a few puffs. i clear my throat
and interrupt the man with the flecked
jacket whos just started up reading his
newspaper.

"excuse me, i dont mean to be rude,
but i wondered if you mite considor
selling that jacket?"

the man with the horse dentures
stairs at my pipe with his yellowey eyes.

"nah, i couldn't sell it, its not
worth anything."

"id pay you for it."

"youed pay money for this?"

"yes."

"i suppose i could."

"no!"

we both turn our heads and see
brincat pushing thru the trestle tables
towards us.

"thats his fucking werk coat, he
cant go selling his werk coat. he aint
nothing else to wear!"

"yes i have, ive got my lammy in my
locker," contradicts old horse dentures.

"no, im not having it! he'd have the
shirt off your back. he's taking fucking
libeties!"

brincat is now standing over me with
his fists bunched up into knots.

"i was only asking . . . i said i'd
pay him for it."

"i told you, it aint for fucking
sale. thats his teddy-boy jacket. what
would you want with it?"

"i like the colours."

"well like away, boy! id rather see
him burn it than sell it to the likes of
you!"

"i really dont mind selling it."

interupts the owner of the jacket.
brincat looks at the man with utter
contempt.

"i spose you can do what you fucking
like, blue." brincat kicks a chair free
and plunks himself down angrily.

the man turns to me. "how much would
you give me?"

"how much do you want?"

"you make an offer."

i straighten my leg, reach my
fingers into my pocket and feel the
change there, "how about one pound 50?"

brincat jumps back up like jack in
the box. "one pound fucking 50? - dose he
look like a fucking mug? you can stick
your fucking one pound 50 where the sun
dont shine, boy! im chucking this jacket
in the ogin after breakfast and you can
whatch it fucking sink, a-men!"

brincat pushes away from the bench,
gets to his feet and storms out of the
caboos, holding furrycat under his arm
and looking hard at me all the way. the
door bangs shut.

the owner of the jacket scruntches
his lips up and sucks on his false teeth.
"dont take any notice of him. he's got a
hart of gold."

i nod. not only dose this fellow
have someone else's dentures in, but he

cant distinguish between an angel and a
deamon. "so you dont want to sell the
jacket?"

"i dont think so. best not to upset
him. plus its good against the rain." and
he stands, turns up the collar of his
jacket and follows the others out.

i sit there for a moment looking
after him. those false teeth of his
looked for all the world like theyd been
carved out of a sheep's collar bone by
some french prisoner of war. the effect
is more like grinning puppets teeth than
anything remotely life-like.

i open up my 1st aid tin and nibble
on the corner of one of my cheese
sandwiches. also in my bag is my book
on fauvisim. i take it out look at the
pictures till everyone else has bogged
off, then its just me sat in there all
alone.

theres no doubt that something is
turning me away from the joys of the
werking life.

✳   ✳   ✳

mattise is the main fellow in that book,
then a few others, one of which has
obviously been taking a good gander at
van gogh.

i shiver and look up. now that all
the toasters are unplugged and the tea
fanny switched itself off its getting
pretty parky in here. the clock on the
wall is pushing 10 too 9 and theres still
no sign of bill. i put my book away and
go poke my head out into the cold gray
lite.

its just as i thort: evryone's gone
to ground, not a sign of life anywere. i
step outside and stair into the distance
till the cold makes my eyes water, but
no matter how hard i flex my peepers bill
still dosnt apear cycling out of the mist
towards me.

would you belive that scearsly 15
minits ago the whole place was teaming
with rough, swearing men clanging their
boots and filling the gutters with
oysters? but now, its just vast and empty
. . . windswept.

you can here a steam engin in the
distence, and a crain teeters along on
its rails, as if it is holding up its
skirts and sceared of the water. other
than that, silence. a group of mattlows
march past, but thats mattlows, not
werkers.

i decide to catch them up and tag
along for a little ways down the ally. i
try to march in time, then the sergeant
sees me, sos i fall out and cut across to
springheels cabin.

as i come past i spy the top of

his head in thru the window then stand
outside the door for a whole minite
hoping from foot to foot, wondering
weather to knock and go in side or head
back over to the caboos and climb under
one of the trestle tables. it really is
chilly around my ankels.

    also, i should have gone to the
loo before venturing outside. i decide
its best to just burst inside and tell
spingheel that ive had 2nd thorts about
this appretiship biusness of theirs.
that the werking life isn't for me after
all and im thinking of taking a break in
the south of france. its not that i dont
appriciate all that has been done for
me, its just that all these fractions,
calculations and angles . . . well, what
do they amount to. in the long run i
mean?

    obviously, a job for life is what
it says it is - a job for life. but is it
nessissarly? who knows when the yard will
be closed down. after all, theres been
rummours in the past, and no job in this
world is copper bottomed. im not saying i
was mislead but there was an eliment of
embellishment. my tools, for example. has
any one seen them? has there ever been a
chit issued? it seams unlikely. and then
there is the question of who is going to
teach me now that bill has concked out.
also, theres the question of algibra
and pythagerius. its not that i abhore
mathmatics either, but the real nub of
the matter is that im an artist not a

lover of improper fractions.

i suck in a deep breath, push the green door open and a great wave of supper heated air pushes over me and evaporates into the hevens above.

springheel is talking on the blower, he looks up, puts his hand over the reciver and vilontly motions for me to shut the door behind me. its pretty toasty in there, 3 bars of a heater banging out and spingheel sat behind his desk with his jacket off.

i cant pretend that im not a little excited that bill didn't come in today. for starters, it means that my werking days, which have already been quite relaxed, really could become something of a luxsoryious holliday.

springheel bangs the resiver back on its cradel and looks me over like im some kind of strange curiosity that has only just come to lite.

"my, my, my, what are we going to do with you, my young master?" and he blinks at me in slow motion, like some kind of bambie.

"i was looking for bill," i explain.

"who?"

"i mean mister cubitt."

"ah, yes, mister cubitt."

"i cant find him, he hasn't come in."

"really, he hasn't come in?"

"no."

"well tell me something else i dont already know," and he smiles smugly with his wet looking lips.

i dutifully smile in acknollegment at springheels excilent joke.

"for your edification, master claudius, that was mister cubitt's wife on the teliphone. so yourll be glade to know that im fully up to date with the situation. as a matter of fact i was just going to send someone over to find you."

springheel flings his wrist out and peers at his watch. "its 10 o'clock now, so what exactly have you been entertaining yourself with all morning?"

"i was waighting."

"waighting? for what, a teligrame from the queen?"

"no, of course not, for bill . . . i mean mister cubitt."

"and when he didn't arrive?"

"i didn't know what time he wasn't arriving. if you see what i mean."

"so in your wisdom you just carrid

on waighting."

i nod. "oh yes, and i was reading my
book. actually i wanted to speak to you
about that . . . and my appretiship ..."

springheel holds up his hand and
shush's me. "that will have to waight,
claudius. theres been enough time
waisting for one day, now we need to get
you out onto site. we'er not paying you
to sit around reading all day, are we."

"no, of course not, but . . . "

springheel looks at me expectantly,
"but what?"

i know what i want to say but it
really is as if a spade loaded with black
mud has been flung into my mouth. i
waggle my toung but no noise comes out, i
shake my head. "nothing."

"excilent, nothing. thats what i
like to hear."

springheel starts flicking irratibly
thru a card index on his desk.

brightstone has a rich new patch of
raw flesh on his neck, where he has been
dragging his razor thru a crop of pimples
that are sprouting their amongst the
purple stubble. one can only imagin this
adds extra vingar to his compassionet
mood.

"is mister cubitt alright?" i
venture.

springheel dosnt even bother looking
up "that would depend on what one means
by allrite. he's been sent away."

    "where to?"

    "over the way."

    "over the way?"

    "across the river."

    i shrug. "is he, bill i mean . . .
is mister cubitt?" and i make a sign with
my eyes.

    "dont be ridiclious, claudius! . . .
at least not yet he isn't. its his blud
pressure, thats all. hes converlessing."

    "how long will he be gone?"

    "who knows. till he's better i
suppose . . . otherwise . . ."

    "otherwise, what?"

    springheel flings the card down and
looks at me, "quit it with all these
questions, im not his keeper, am i!" and
he picks up the card again and starts
reading.

    i waight for a respectfull moment
then ask another question. "whos going to
teach me, now that bill - mister cubitt,
i mean - is ill?"

    "thats presisly what i am trying to
sort out, claudius, if your'll just shut

up for 5 minits!"

"i could go home, i suppose. if im
not needed that is."

springheel ignores my suggestion and
starts rummidging around in a 2nd box of
green coloured cards. these ones have red
typing on them.

"or i could go out on the island and
finish my carving."

"what carving?" springheel cocks
his head like a curious dog.

"nothing really. a profile or
two. practice really. one of red cloud.
and a bust of van gogh, then theres my
reclining admril."

"reclining admril! does the admril
know about this?"

"well its not him in particular,"
i correct myself, "its more of 'a'
reclining admril."

"i hope you haven't been out on the
island unsupervised?"

"only on my lunch break."

"your not to be out on the island at
all! its a restricted arear. theres stuff
out there. real bad stuff!"

"the mustach has come off the bust
of van gogh. i hit some shale."

"yes, very interesting im sure."
and springheel continues flicking thru
the cards. "theres no other mason in the
yard. the bricky's refuse to have you on
site . . . so what the hell am i ment to
do with you!"

"of course ile do anything required
of me. even if it is against union
rules." i add, helpfully.

"theres no union in here!" says
springheel with some venom. "this yard
has a royal charter!" he looks back down
at his card index and starts flicking
away again with gaining force and
irratation.

"that idiot johnson say's he
wouldn't put up with an apprentice mason
labouring for his brickys! you can take
it from me, that was my dession, not his.
the bluddy nurve!"

i nod in agreement, which seams to
agitate springheel even more.

"i was just agreeing with you." i
explain.

springheel smiles ironicly. "you
have a rite, apparently, to be taught
the skill that you have been apprenticed
too, and i am not going to controvine
that directive. oh no! because it is a
government directive. not because some
upstart chargehand starts dictating to
me!

"damn and blast you, claudius!
what possessed you to choose stonemasonry
in the 1st place! no one applys for
stonemasonry, and i mean no one!
you could of chosen anything else,
boilermaker! . . . electrician! . . . "

"have my tools arrived yet?" i
interrupt him.

"im sorry?"

"my tools. they promised me my own
set of tools."

it is possible to see the colour
rising in springheels face. "ive already
told you, a chit has to be issued."

"yes, but arnt you ment to issue
it?"

"dont come the old acid with me,
claudius! go to the store. thats the
place to get any tools that need to be
issued."

"no, im serrious."

"its not my department. your'll need
to speak to mister cubitt."

"but he's not here."

"then go to the stores!"

"but bill said that i had to get
a chit from you to take to them to
authorise them to order them in."

springheel holds up his hand and
shakes his head. "no, no, no! forget it.
im not interested. go and interrogate
somebody else. ive got my own headaches!"

i look at him. really, at the top of
his head.

"is it alright if i use the toilet?"

"no, it is not alright. this toilet
is for staff and charge hands. go across
the yard, theres a facility in the werk
hut for people like you."

"ile just go over there then," and i
go as if to leave.

"and where do you think your going?"

"i thort maybe i should just stay
in the caboos and practice my drawing."

springheel really perks up, comes
from behind his desk and puts his face
very close to mine. from this range its
possible to see the dots in his nose and
smell his oniony breath. i have to look
at his raw neck intead of his eyes. then
i have to look at his tie, which has a
lillac hue and yellow dots.

"your not here to doodle, claudius,
but werk!"

"just until you find something else,
i mean."

"oh, dont you worry, claudius, ile
find something nice and jucey for you."

"honestly, i dont mind waighting in the hut. it wouldn't be any trouble."

"oh, im sure it wouldn't be any trouble!"

"just until mister cubitt gets better."

"he's a milingerer, claudius. you know what a milingerer is?"

"someone who's gone to see the ships?"

"a flipping skiver!"

"i thort it was his blud presure?"

"you know as well as i do that theres nothing rong with cubitts blud pressure, his just swinging the lead!"

this isn't strickly true, as i saw one of bills fountains with my own eyes, but i can see that its best not to contradict springheel in his present mood.

"so when will he come back?"

springheel turns away and kicks at the leg of his desk. "tomorrow! next week! next month! never! im damned if i know." suddenly he snatches up the telephone and diels a number. "head office in deal, they'll know what to do with you. perhaps you can go to canterbury and werk on the cathedral. they at least have stonemasons!"

it really is terrificly exciting
being stood here, whatching springheels
addams apple poping in and out as he
gases on the blower. i try to listen
in, but only getting one side of the
conversation its hard to follow, i get
the impression that the cathedrial is a
no-no. springheels tone grows more and
more strained as he fails to palm me
off as a labourer for 1st one bunch of
loafers, then another.

so this is the rude awakening ive
been promised.

springheel slams down the reciver.

"ile go and waight over in the
caboos, shall i?"

"you stay rite where you are!"
springheel narrows his eyes at me, "your
not going anywhere till this is sorted
out once and for all."

i stand there watching him as he
passes from his desk to the doorway,
where he violently about turns and
marches back again. finnaly he turns on
me and shouts at me to get out.

chapter 12

god sends nuts to people without teeth

once i hear a rumour of my next berth i
cycle out into the sea wall and squint my
eyes thru the drizzel.

the castle, for thats what the
building in fact was, was not so much
shrowded in mist as buried in dence fog,
with only an occasional turrit drifting
in and out of view.

it certenly looks mysterious over
there. 2 turrets, and a wooden palacade
stretching across the mud and out into
the river. from here you can just pick
out a row of little castleations, built
to welcome the inquisitive dutchmen who
come sniffing about looking for ships of
the line to tow home and boast of their
bravery.

fact: if the yard bothered to lay on
a row boat i could be at werk with 2 good
pulls of an ore.

※　　　　　　　※　　　　　　　※

to the castle.

the van, with the clutch screaming,
climbs up the hill and into the muddy car
park, it headlamps showing as pale discs.

"gustov!"

i here a voice calling thru the fog.

i slam the door and watch as the
van pulls away and then the voice comes
again, indistinct, far off, piping like a
lost bird of the marshes. just thinking
this makes me smile to myself - a pre-
historich archeoptricx calling my name,
indeed. i stamp my feet and do a liitle
circit of the mudy pools of the car park.

calling it a carpark is one thing,
it actually being one is another.
admitedly, theres some tyer tracks in
the mud, and theres some evidence that
somebody once emptied a bag of gravel
in this trecherious marsh, but a more
truthfull discription would be 'a boggy
clearing in the woods', rather than the
grandios title of 'the sir thomas hawkins
memorial carpark'.

"gustov!"

thou the far end of their carpark
is clothed in fog i can still make out
the branches of some distent trees, and a
small, almost hidden gap with a footpath
leading away, down thru some scrub. this
must be where the voice is coming from.

"gustov!" there it goes again. a
distent bird cry, lonsome and felorn.

"gustov!"

thats what old springheel rote
down, licking at his pencil: 'claudius',
followed by 'gustov' in the next column.
he labours over it, letter by letter.

"someone will meet you, in the
carpark. a fellow named frank. tell him
i sent you . . . the sir thomas hawkins
memorial car park, you got that?"
springheel checks his time piece. "the
van will be here any minit, you'd best
wait outside. we'll call once we get word
from mister cubitt. dont forget, ask
for frank, an old fellow, gray wiskers,
wearing a cap, 2 hairs growing out the
end of his nose."

i stand around in the fog, flapping
my arms about. "gustov!"

how does he know my name, this
cocatoo? i keep walking into the mists.
up a head i see a large oak tree with a
scearcrow stood benith. it has its arms
outstretched and a real mangel-wursel for
a head. as i watch it calls out my name,
then pauses to make a wolf-whistle, befor
drapping its hand through a patch of
nettles.

i call hello and step forward. the
scearcrow turns to me.

"are you gustov?"

"yes." i answer.

"good. ive been sent up from
the castle to guide you in across the
marshes. its the fog, awfull thick. you
dont want to loose your way, it can be
pretty tretcherious. plus theres been
talk of smugglers a-foot, and they are
not nice people to run into. my names
frank, by the way."

i say hello. im not really sure
if frank expects me to belive his fairy
tails, but i nod anyway.

"excuse me," and frank reaches into
a great clump of stingers and swaths his
arm about in there, rite up to the elbow.
"its my arthritis, see. i spent too many
years at sea. its the damp," he explains.
"there you are!" he holds out his old
man's claw for me: sinuous, gnarled
knuckels, purple veins and little white
stings, hundreds of them one on top of
the other, all over his mitt and rite up
his arm.

"doctors? doctors? who needs 'em!
ive mended it myself." and he flexes his
hand to check its still werking properly
before stuffing it in his pocket and off
he hobbles through the bushes. "ile teach
you how to tap dance if you fancy. come
on, dont dawdle!" i have to jog along to
keep up.

"so youre the new boy are you?"

"yes, i spose so."

257

"bricky?"

"no, stonemason."

frank stops, whistels softly and
looks me up and down. "my, you dont get
many of those. not these days." and he
heads off again. "there ain't no call for
'em. theres none over here you know, not
for years! it dont look like youre gonna
be learning much, does it? oh, bugger my
leg! pardon my french. what did you say
your name was?"

"you were just callin my name,
remember?"

"was i? oh yes, of course i was.
gustov, gustov, gustov. i knew it was,
i remember. thats quite an impressive
monika you've got there."

"its from my grandad. he was
fighting the white russians . . ."

frank holds up his hand and cuts me
off mid sentence. "listen!" and he cocks
an ear. i listen out - nothing. then i
here screaming. frank shakes his head,
"no, thats nothing. a ferrits got a jack
rabit, thats all." and off we go again.

"its a pretty cushy set-up we've got
out here, gustov." frank taps the side
of his nose. "remotes the word for it.
out of sight, out of mind, if you get my
drift" and he winks and smiles, another
set of moulded tombs. "its what we call a
cushy billet. keep yourself to yourself,

258

and just as long as youre not caught
taking the piss, its a job for life!"
franks whole face beams in a grin of
sunny contentment.

   this 'its a job for life!' and 'dont
get caught taking the piss' seam to be
the dockyard mantras.

   "here we are, this is it." frank
pulls up short in front of an old
corrugated hut which still has a coat of
cammoflauge painted on it.

   "morning tea break," he explains and
nods towards the door, "morning tea break
in there." frank hunches his shoulders
and blows on his claw. "look at that, its
closing again!" he holds up his hand then
slaps it hard on his thigh.

   "you introduce yourself when we go
in. ivors the chief sherang. he likes to
know who's who."

   i nod, and then we enter.

   theres a lot of hot air blowing
between the old lags. 3 of them, sat over
by the window, are talking and objecting.
another 2, with heads in their morning
papers, bearly look up. frank nudges me
and points his eyes at ivor, who seems
to be gaurding the tea fanny. i step
forward.

   "excuse me, im gustov. mister
springheel jack sent me."

"ivor looks me in the eye. "you mean mister brightstone."

"yes, sorry. mister brightstone."

"well, im the charge hand, you can call me ivor, everybody else does. oi. you lot, this heres gustov."

the heard lift their heads from their respective arguments and nod at me: mouthfuls of tea and half-eaten biscuits. its quite a wax werks, old solders and dryed prunes mostly, left here to die quitly, in this tucked away place.

one espesherly wrinkled face peers at me through his thick speckticels and dunks his biscuit. without taking his eyes off me he manoeuvres the biscuit towards his gob, folds back his lips, exposses his purple gums and sucks it in.

"fuck mine, thats hot!" and he looks round and laughs to the room, but no one bothers to join him in his merryment.

"thats fred," says ivor.

i say hello.

fred's lips pinch together, some biscit juice runs down his chin and his toung comes out and chases it: no teeth, just gums. and the whole contents of his mouth on show; yellowish liquid and the dangly bit swimming about in it at the back. finally he closes his trap and wipes his mush with his sleeve. "bleeding

lovan audence, but he has to make do with
only me. nothing like a good brew and a
dunk. er, graham?"

"who the blinking hell's graham?"
asks frank.

"i thort you said his name was
graham."

"my eye i did, i said his name was
gustov. get that in your bean, you old
fool. i should know co's im the one that
trappsed up the soddin car park to fetch
him."

fred put his serious face on.
"gustov?"

"yes," i nod quickly.

"so whats your party piece?"

"he's an apprentice," puts in ivor.

"apprentice what? nut-juggler!"

"hes a blinking stonemason, ain't
yer gus," says frank.

fred pushes his glasses back on his
nose. "well what we gonna do with him? we
dont have no use for stonemasons here.
youd better go back to where you come
from, sonny!"

ive always been told to be polite,
so i smile. i give him a little grimace.

"no, i told him, not for . . .

what?" says frank.

"years!"

"yeah, must be years."

"decades more like!"

"thats what i said to him, gustov,
i said, you ain't gonna learn much here,
son. we haven't got any, we dont need any
and we haven't had one since gawd knows
when."

"decades!" says ivor, slapping his
palm down on the bench.

"so what did they send him here for
then?" asks fred.

"beats me," replys ivor, "but why
do they do any number of things? because
they dont know their arses from their
elbows, thats why. order spaghetti,
they'll serve you bleeding bandages!"

frank and fred look at him askance.

"well, he ain't gonna learn much
about fucking masonry here. i can tell
you this much. you done any bricking
sonny? brickwork? he can learn some of
that."

one old fellow, sat in the corner,
who they refer to as killer, fixes me
with a curious look, or rather stairs off
over my shoulder, sos i cant tell if hes
actually looking at me at all. "so wheres
you from, son?"

"wake up, killer. his from the dockyard, incha, gus?" butts in frank, "they just dropped him off in the van."

"the dockyard? it would have been quicker for him to swim."

killer has got a glass eye, you can tell because it has a slightly different hue, plus it dosnt seam to move a great deal, whilest the other one roves around feeling you all over.

"i walked it in the winter of 47, clean across the ice" states killer.

"you never did!" retorts frank.

"no joshing. i walket it!" re-states killer.

"bollox you did!" says fred.

"dont listen those wallys, dont know thier arse's from their elbows. i walked from upnor, clear across the river the whole winter of 47."

"you came to werk on the ferry, same as everyone else."

"your partly correct, frank . . ."

"partly correct? im bang on, killer!"

the one called killer turns to me "there was a ferry but the top brass, in their infinite wisdom, scrapped the fucker back in the 1960s."

"aye, that they did, killer. now you 'ave to swim!"

"thats what im telling the lad! i just opens my door and walks clear across. yep, i walkt to werk, shanks's poney!" and killer pulls up his trousers bottoms and shows me his varicus vains. "not bad for an old boy, er?"

"for gawds sake put 'em away," crys ivor. "christ, the boy dosnt want to see your disgusting old gams, they look like bludy blue cheese! let the lad sit down and give him a mug of tea someone. did you bring your mug, gustov?"

"ive got the one on my flask," i venture.

"never mind that, give him the spare . . . its a bit chipped, but wash it out and it'le be good as new. you dont want tea out of a plastic cup - tastes bludy horrible!" ivor dunks the mug in the tea fanny." he plonks a brew down infront of me, "there you go, beggars cant be choosers."

fred stretches his arms and legs out with an exaggerated groan, "well, i cant sit about here all day gassing. some of us have werk to do." and stands and pulls his cap down hard over his dome. "well, isn't there werk to be done?"

no one else budges, then as one they lift their mugs and take a deep sup.

"ivor, youre the gaffer. tell them theres work to be done!"

"for christs sakes, put a sock in it" mutters killer.

ivor sucks his teeth. "its twenty past, fred. we start at half past. its only twenty past now."

"not by my watch, it ain't!"

"has the boy got a watch? ask him," pipes up killer.

they all put their mugs down and look at me expectantly.

theres a moments silence, then it dawns on me: i understand what im supposed to do. i ment to look at my watch and spill my tea all down my front. i decide that i have little choice; that it would be rong to dissapoint them. even thou im not wearing a watch i turn my rist as if to look at the time and the tea goes down my leg.

"20 past." i say.

theres a moments silence, then the hole caboos exploads in to laughter. they rock back and forth dabbing at their eyes and howling in each others faces. it really does seam to be terribly amusing and even i have to smile at my stupidity.

"we had you there, son, we had you there!" shouts killer, and they all start baying like hounds. fred even acts out my

movements: a little mime of the action of
my rist and the small amount of tea that
went down my trouser leg. killer looks on
clapping his hands in glee, his real eye
darting about like a blue tit, whilest
the glass one stairs dead.

in their minds i really am drentched
to bone in scalding tea. everytime they
look up and see my wane face they crease
up into new fits of mirth. apparently it
really is the funnyist thing that has
ever happened in the history of the tea
hut.

fred sits back down and slaps his
thighs. "oh, my gawd, you should have
seen your face! we had you good and
proper!" he takes his glasses off and
dabs at his eyes with an old spotted
hanky.

i smile sheepishly round the room.
so this is how gracious they are when
you play along with one of their excilent
games.

"your all rite son," and ivor slaps
my shoulder. "his allrite, isn't he?"
and they all nod and lift their tin mugs
to me, welcoming me into their retarded
family.

with only exagirating the point a little
it could be said that the big story in
the caboos that morning was about a
certen incedent that had taken place the
nite before. many column inches had been
devoted to it acroos the pages of the
national newspapers. in short, the air
was throbbing with ritious indignation.

fred jabs his sausagy fingers at the
headlines. "look at it! read it! whats
that all about!" demands fred. again he
raps at the paper with his fat finger
tipps, spreading out like little spades,
nicotine stained, the nails broken and
chipped.

"there ain't no need for it, thats
certain." agrees killer.

"the worlds gone doolally!" states
fred.

"listen to this," a voice pipes up
from the corner. "it says that this bloke
here kicked his tv set in. 150 quid's
worth! what do you make of that?"

"the man needs his bleeding head
felt," says frank, "i'd of just switched
it off."

"exactly!"

"150 quid? christ on a bike!"

fred turns to a younger looking man
who is sat quitly filling in a crossword,
"ron, did you see it? . . . ron . . .

ron!"

the one called ron looks up. "what?"

"these punk rockers swaearing on the
telly, last nite?"

"no. wurst luck!"

theres a silence before they all
realise that they should laugh.

i take a sip on my brew: super-sweet
made with condensed milk. it makes your
suck teeth ache that stuff - liquid iron,
gluey with leaves in it, a little pool of
them at the bottom.

"you like your brew, lad?" thats
ivor speaking. "condensed milk, that is.
did you see the telly?"

i shake my head.

"its in all the papers! they only do
it for the publicity you know, they ain't
stupid."

"stupid fuckers!" interjects fred.

"they ain't stupid," repeats ivor,
"the stupid one is the idiot who kicked
his own tv screen in. now that is what i
call thick."

theres a mooing of agreement and
they all lift their cups and sup as one.

fred takes off his glasses, gives
them a quick wipe and pops them back on

again. he starts moving his lips, getting
ready to speak.

"here, ivor, you know the glass bit
inside the telly, not the screen, but the
bit inside?"

"you mean the tube?" asks ivor.

"yes, thats it. the tube. yeah, the
tube. if that gets busted it explodes and
sends out tiny splinters of glass for
miles around." fred shows us how small
between his nicotine stained fingers.
"minute," he carries on, "tiny."

"implodes," corrects ivor. "they
dont explode, they implode, its a
vacuum."

"do what?"

"the tube of a telly. it dosnt
explode, it implodes. theres a vacuum
inside and a vacuum implodes. the glass
dosnt go out, it gos in."

"so what's the fucking difference?"

"the difference is, is that it
goes inwards, like in space. thats the
difference."

"yeah, but then it goes out again
after it meets in the middle."

"maybe it does," says ivor,
doubtfully.

"well, thats what im bludy-well

saying, isn't it!" and he looks to frank
to back him up.

frank shines his chompers at me,
gleaming in his wrecked mug. "the boy
likes his tea. condensed milk that is,
gustov. like we used to drink in the war.
none of your moden, fresh milk rubbish."

and he nods at me. encouraging me to
take another sip. i feel that i have to.
i swallow through the tea leafs, bitter-
sweet, clinging, and give him a 1/2
smile over the chipped enamel.

one day it will be my turn to
say how the world was when i was young
and so be able to instruckt young
whippersnappers about the uslessness of
their moden day living.

"a lovely brew that, boy! naffi tea,
just like we had in the war."

"naffi tea, my arse! naffi tea was
piss!" say fred, the one with the deepest
wrinkles.

"army tea," continues frank,
"naffi tea, berlin 1945, i was there, he
wasn't," and he nods in fred's general
direction and leans in, confiding with me
in a loud whisper, "still sucking on his
mother's tit, he was!"

"i bloody heard that, frank bludy
scrimshore! dont you listen to him, son -
what ever your name is - the only reason
i wasn't there was 'cos i was invalided

out at dunkquirk. and he bludy knows it!"

"dunkquirk my elbow, you were
skiving in the dockyard!"

"1939, i was a regular in the bef!"

"im telling the boy my war memories,
not your fairy tales!" frank turns back
to me, "after the war, berlin 1946, you
could stand your spoon up in it it was
that thick. i went all the way, from
normandy to the elb. helpt liberate
belson. there was this girl in there who
kept a newspaper up her whats-it. they
didn't have pockets so where else is she
ment to stow it?"

"but the tea was piss!" interjects
fred.

"they had these birds in berlin
clearing rubble out of the roads. all the
men were dead so they used women. big old
boilers they were, and they could piss
standing up, 6 feet stright into a milk
bottle without spilling a drop."

"dont listen to him, he's making it
up."

"they pulled themselves out through
the front of their overalls and pissed
just like a bloke - standing up - rite
in the middle of the street in broad
daylite. 6 feet, straight as an arrow,
no squatting. then theyed just tuck them
self's away and carry on stacking bricks,
like it was the most natural thing in the

world."

"bolloxs, did they!"

"bolloxs youself!"

that was fred, no teeth, just the
gums. the upper jaw shrunken in and his
lips gathered up under his nose in a
wedge.

"total bollox! dont believe a word
he tells you. has he told you how he
swam to gibralter yet? you ever had your
pisser pulled? well his pulling it now!
thats rite isn't it, ivor?"

"your not dragging me into it."

"well, he's talking out his arse
and he knows it! naffi tea's the same the
world over, gnat's piss! oi, ron, ron!
you did your national service, gnat's
piss, wasn't it? - naffi tea."

ron scratches at the end of his
nose with his pecil, folds the paper
thoughtfully, then places it down on the
table, drains his tea and stands.

"come on, gustov, its 20 to 10, time
to get out on site."

i look at ron, then to ivor. ivor
nods for me to follow. "you go with ron,
your'll be on the walls today."

"on the walls?"

"yes."

"you mean outside?"

"yes, outside. you go with ron,
he'll show you the ropes."

i get up and follow ron out. 'on the
walls' is obviously a term im ment to be
familiar with.

the others lift their eyes from
their mugs of tea and watch us go. there
seams to be no urgency for them to go
'out on the walls', and i see ivor
filling the tea fanny again before the
door closes.

"oi, put the lump in the hole! you
wernt born in a bleeding barn, were you!"

we step out into a wall of wet fog.
it licks me all over, looking for the gap
between my socks and trouser bottoms . .
. ron stomps off up the gravel path and i
put a trot on to catch up with him.

we pass under the walnut trees,
then you see the tower looming thru the
fog like a thumb dissapearing into the
clouds.

in under a gateway then theres a
small courtyard and the keep wall.

ron unties a plank from the bottom
of a ladder and scampers off up the
scaffold. 1, 2, 3, 4 levels, playing
follow my leader. one more level to go,
and then suddenly our heads brake free of
the pea soup into blinding sunlite. one

moment we'er groping thru gray smoke the
next everything goes golden: countless
hexaganels of refrected lite, shooting
out their sparkels and up into gods world
with angels singing.

we stand, a great sea of white fog
spread benieth us, covering the river,
the dockyard and the towns beyond. a
crane juts his nose into the air; the
cathedrail spire - and us sat on our
perch, on top of everything so to speak.

"this is the inner wall . . .
you see down there? are you afraid of
heights? dont worry, you'll get used to
it soon enough . . . dont look down,
least not after the fogs cleared anyway,
otherwise!"

as ron says 'otherwise!' he makes
his eyes slant sideways, his head tilts
back and his mouth falls open. i look at
him playing possom, a curiouse effect,
almost theatrical.

"it used to bother me," says ron,
"but not anymore. i dropped a cheese and
pickle sandwidge over the edge once,
almost took me with it! . . . anyway, you
look smart enough, not that looks are
anything to go by . . . you know how old
this castle is?"

"its elisabethan, isn't it?"

ron looks at me and nods, "yes,
elisabethan. very good, im impressed."

and then i cant stop myself and have
to brag about helping rite a history of
the forts whilest i was a skool boy. "me
and my friend fish published it. i did
the drawings."

ron narrows his eyes. "i see we have
a propper little historian on our hands!"

"they built this castle after the
dutch raid. the cheese eaters burned the
fleet and when the dockyard askt for
volenteers to help fight them only 2
werkers came forward."

"so youre an artist as well as a
published historian." and ron turns away
and starts coiling a loose roap. i relise
that ive over stepped the mark and tail
off.

"anyway, some of us have werk to
do." ron looks at my face to be sure
ive shut up. "you see the wall here?
see where its bowed? if we dont take
that out the whole lot'll be coming down
on someonce bonce! i suppose you could
make a sketch of it, but that wont help
the wounded, will it. so take all these
stones out . . . like this . . . see?
the morters shot, like dust . . . here
she comes, thats it, now bung it in the
bucket. when its full you lower over
the side, then you nip down there and
lay them out in a row on the grass. and
number them with this pice of chalk as
you go. if any get busted you knock us
up a new one the same dimensions. only

roughly, it dosnt need to be precise. so
if they crumble make sure you keep the
bits. theres a pile of stone over by the
main entrance. and dont forget to number
them, each stone, with this chalk . . .
lay them in rows just as they come out,
with this code, thats the prefix and
thats the number. you got all that? . . .
say if you dont follow me."

    ron looks at his rist watch, "right
then, let's get started, it'll be tea
break in 3/4's of an hour."

    thats how we werk: in between tea
breaks and the fog and the sky: drapped
in mist and drizzling. but if you can
ignore the cold and damp - and celibrate
the fact that we are holding the same
rotting stone in our hands as our tudor
forefathers - then its possible to see
that there is yet something magical about
it all.

    and this man with a boys face comes
down from the big estate with his black
labradour, galloping out in front. ron
tells me that hes the gamekeeper, which
would explain why he wears a tweed cap.
ron lifts out crumbling rocks and me
lowering them down in my bucket, and the
dog wagging his tail.

    to describe this gamekeeper as a
boy/man is mearly to confirm that he had
the face of a freakish kid.

    it must be that he takes the dog
out walkies every morning, as we see them

about 10.30 ish, mosing about between
the stones, apperently waighting for the
midmorning tea break. yes, they time
their apperrence from out the bushs with
the tea and nibby.

me and ron shinny down the ladders.
the dog sees's us coming and starts
barking, they have a head start on us. we
race them to the caboos but when we come
in the door they'er all sat there calm as
you like, the boy/man with a steaming mug
of hot tea in front of him and the dog
under the table, thumping his tail and
panting his toung.

that dog was soft and used to
drink my tea. as soon as everybody
starts gassing i slip my mug under the
table: 3 laps and its gone. dogface had
a taste for all that condensed milk . .
. swirling in tea leaves . . . orange,
heavy, with a whiff of iron: the spoon
stood upright, and then he bolts it down
in one go. good boy!

really black, that dog was, with
a little bit of chocolate in him . . .
friendly, good natured, with a taste for
franks foul brew.

     ✻   ✻   ✻

all week we keep on it: climbing the
ladders and pulling out the broken

stones.

its some lookout post we've got up
here, a crows nest on top of the world.
the fog burns off about 10 ish and you
can see everything revieled: all the
comings and goings. over the river into
the dockyard, little ships, the grounds
below, the gate house, then the lane and
the carpark, the walls and the village
beyond.

you can even see into the squire's
estate. and theres the gamekeeper, way
over there, checking on his pheasants,
almost out of sight . . . knelt down in
the bushes . . . and his dog, miniature
in the far distance. you watch them
larking about . . . dogface has some fun,
pouncing and prancing over the moors and
through the heather. like a little match
stick dog, so far away it makes your eyes
ache.

"you see, over there, thats the
west tower, thats where queen elizabeth
1st took a shite."

i look at ron and smile at his joke.

"its nothing to laugh at, im not
ribbing you. i thort you'ed know all
about that, what with your history
ritting."

"know about what?"

"good queen bess. when she came down
here to open the castle - well, she'd

have to take a dump, wouldn't she?"

i nod. "yes, i spose so. i hadn't really thort about it."

"honest to god, the long drops still in there. when i 1st came to werk here the tudor shit house was still intact."

i take ron's word for it. after all, who am i to contradict him? but it all sounds a little speculative to me. theres no real hard evidence, but theres no doubt that good queen bess, as he calls her, came here to open the castle.

"they had all sorts of junk in that tower, a few years back. stacked to the rafters with momentoes from rouks drift. zulu shield, those little pears, head dresses, rifels, the lot. the engineers brought it back with them. then one day this geeser comes down from the mod and tells us to drag down the beach and burn the lot. they wanted the space or something. we wernt allowed to save a thing. 'if we catch any of you tacking so much as single lions tail', they said 'your'll be fired on the spot and no pension!' so we do as he says and stick a match under it and puff, up it goes in smoke! . . . hello, who's this?"

ron stands and peers over the edge of the scaffold, down into the courtyard bellow.

"look, here comes fred. you haven't seen this yet, have you?"

i stand next to ron and look down
through the criss-cross scaffolding,
planks and ladder runs.

i see him, below us, a little to
the left, with his hands jammed in his
pockets and his lid pulled down over his
ears, hobbling between one wall and the
next.

"he ain't got no teeth you see, and
he wont wear dentchurs either. had all
his teeth out in one go on the national
health. he wont werk no more on account
of his sciatica, so ivor sends him out
collecting litter, so at least it looks
like his buisy . . . now watch him. look,
you see what hes gumming, toffee brittle
that is, he always eats that, but he
ain't got no teeth, so he has to gum it.
and he cant eat the nuts, on account that
his gums are to soft . . . look . . .
see, he cant chew it, he has to suck it."

i listen to ron and pretend to be
interested. i nod at the rite moments and
remember to smile in amusement at each
new enthrawling reverlation.

"thats it! look, he's taken another
lump out of his pocket. toffee brittle
that is."

i can just make fred out. he's
wearing a blue anorack and a cap. he
sticks his paw into his pocket, takes
something out, breaks a piece off and
tosses it into his mouth.

"he cant eat the nuts - no teeth you
see. and he won't wear false ones, says
they irritate his gums. dosnt stop him
woofing down sausages, mind!

"now look, can you see them, down
there on the wall! there they go!"

i look to the wall. there seams to
be some ivy growing there, but i cant see
anything else in particular.

"there, theres a dozen of them!"

i rub my eyes, but nothing.

"not there, over there! they've
moved by the cedar tree now."

i shrug.

"are you blind or something, theres
at least 15 of them . . . look, his
little friends are gathering, they're
following him!"

i really look double hard. i flex my
retinas, but there is nothing to see. it
really is as if ron is having me on.

"over there! they've moved again!"

all i see is fred siting directly
below us. i see his cap and the tops of
his ears moving as his gums pound away at
the toffee, but nothing else.

"there they go! they're lined up,
ready for action!"

fred cracks off another lump of
toffee and tosses it in his gob.

now i see them: a whole row of
little brown house sparrows, sitting in
a row along the top of the wall. rons
talking about sparrows! now i get it, i
was looking for something alltogether
bigger, maybe a row of sea eagles or
something.

i can see their little brown heads
bobbing from side to side, watching
freds every move - his chomping jaws -
inquisitive, expectant.

fred stands, brushes himself down
and walks on a few paces. the sparrows
ruffle their feathers, flap off, then
settle again, a few yards on. chirpy
little fellows, following fred, just to
one side and behind, shadowing him from a
safe distence.

"he's going to do it any minute.
dont blink your eyes, not even for a
split second . . . they're following him,
their not stupid . . . you know when
fred's coming because you see his little
flock of followers dancing in the air."

fred checks over his shoulder,
sucks his lips back over his gums and out
they come: a great fan of nuts, denuded,
flying through the air in a jet of
spittle. hot and wet; in little groups;
single ones; all smeared with juice.
freds eyes bulge behind his glasses, he
shakes his jowls, puts his tongue behind

them and they shoot out like buck shot, scattering to left and rite.

the peanuts fall amongst all the individual blades in a neat little semi-circle. and the flock of little brown ones descend. they hop off the wall as one and follow their beaks, scrutinising in amongst the individual blades. i can see their little soft forms, about 10 or 20 of them, a mad flurry of the little brown ones: the eating of the nuts.

* * *

next morning its proper raining so we dont go up on the wall, and instead frank teaches me a bit of tap dancing in the old guard room.

to call it proper tap dancing is a streatch, basicly you toe-heal-toe as you walk across the room. franks not so fast on account of his gammy leg, but he can speed it up a bit on one foot to make the sound of a galloping horse.

after that we stand in the door way looking out into the rain.

"sod this for a game of solders, lets get back over the hut and get a brew on, it must be about 1/2 past by now."

we duck out into the rain.

when you walk into that caboos
it really is like happening across the
cast of an ancient tea party thats been
mummified in some subterainian catacomb.
you look at their faces and its hard to
belive their still drawing breath.

sitting amongst these old solders
and merlingerers, i like to imagin that i
liven the place up a little. naturally,
what with having only just got my feet
under the table, as it were, it wouldn't
be rite to puff my neck out too much,
or declair openly that my presence adds
a certain youthfulness to an otherwise
dusty and tomb-like atmosphere, but i bet
its a lot nicer now that im here.

also, of course, i make my pencil
drawings, sketching in their crumbing
mugs as they feed their faces with fruit
cake that my mother baked to bring in.
then, one by one, they raise a cheek from
the wooden bench to let go a corker.

"you know who i had on the blower
this morning? - here, gustov, this
concerns you - only old brightstone." all
eyes turn on ivor.

"springheel jack! whats that bugger
want with us?" asks frank.

"he's checking in on the lad, of
course." answers ivor.

"but he's not actually coming here,
is he?"

"yes, after dinner."

"today?"

"thats what im telling you."

frank turns to the others, "why for's that barstard coming over here? ile tell you why for, to snoop about, thats why for!"

"dont get your knickers in a twist, its no big deal. we'll just batten down the hatches as normal and keep to winward of that barstard. but remember, dont answer any question, leave any talking to me. that goes for the lot of yous, espesherly the boy." ivor nods at me, "so young gustov, you make sure you keep it buttoned, dont let him catch you swinging the lead. ron, make sure it looks like your keeping his nose too the grind stone."

ron arches his eyebrows at me to re-afirm ivors orders.

yes, i am told to listen and made concious that it is because of my youth that i am sent to the top of the scaffold to experence the cold and damp at 1st hand.

ivor basicly rattles the cage and hurds us out of the caboos.

"okey-dokey, everybody show a leg and get out on site. come on, sup up and get out."

the rains praticly stopped. me and
ron saunter over to the keep. as usual
ron unties the plank on the ladder and
skips up the 1st flight. then he pulls
up short. "sod it! i forgot me sarnies.
would you go and grab 'em for us, gustov,
theres a good lad."

i head back down the lader and walk
across the lawn. ron shouts from the top
of the scaffold, "there in my bag on the
back of my chair." i wave and carry on.

i push open the door and put
the lite on. theres a lot of smells
compeating for dominence in that little
tin hut of ours: margerine, bacon, tea
and farts.

theres rons duffel bag. i pick it up
and head for the door. im just going to
click the lite off when i have an idear.

i go sit down, get my sketch book
out and start to draw a little still life
of the unwashed mugs and a sause bottle.

actually, i get quite excited.
basicly its my fault that old springheel
has come sniffing about. now, if i sit
here and waight for him then he wont have
to go and bother the others and i can
just grab my gear, jump in the van and
be off without the others knowing. how
mysterious that would be.

also, of course, springheel will
catch me sketching. imagine the surprise
on his face when he sees my hidden

tallents. he'll premote me, most likely.
or at least give me the sack. and who
knows, he mite even commission me to do
a portrate of his wife and children.
that certenly isn't beyond the relms of
possibility. afterall, new talent has to
be 'un earthed', i belive the term is,
from somewhere.

i here the door open. my moment has
come and i have been discovered at last.
i pause a moment, for effect, then look
up from my sketch book. only its not
spingheel stood there, towering in the
doorway with hands on his hips, but ron.

"what the fucking hell do you think
you are doing!"

"drawing." i answer deffensivly.

"i can fucking see that! you realise
that brightstones here already? hes been
up on the wall looking for you. i thort i
told you to grab my sarnis."

"i did, but i thort id make a quick
sketch."

"a quick sketch, my arse! you know
he's only waighting to catch us out so's
he can give us all the heave-ho!"

i smile apologeticly. i can see now
that i have made a mistake. yes, ron is
annoyed with me, you could almost say he
was incondecent with anger, or somehow
'beside himself'. both terms exist and
have been applied in such situations

before.

"what if he catchs you loafing
in here? who gets the jawbation? yours
fucking truly! and ile have to defend you
and, wollop, ive lost my job! thank you
very much! good bye any early retirment!
good bye pension! and good bye mg sports
car!"

i nod, stand and put my sketch
book in my scran bag. yes, of course
ron is rite. after all, there really is
his early retirment to consider, and as
he says - the dreamed of sports car. is
that all to be thrown away on behalf of
a half-wit with delusions of artistic
grandure? on behalf of a boy who sits
around doodling in the tea huts of hell
like a great, blessed sissy, rather than
taking to the ramparts and pretending to
look like a man who scorns soft hands.

      ✳   ✳   ✳

we walk back over to the wall. ron spys
old springheel lolloping along. "look at
him, the great university ponce! here,
hold this." ron puts a set square in my
hand. "here he is, mister brightstone. he
was just fetching a set square from my
donkey box."

i step over the little lawn to
admire springheels shaving rash. i pick

my way betwen the rows of busted stones.

apparently bill's resurfaced, the
van's waighting. i have to bid my fond
farewells, pack my flask and fire my arse
back to the dockyard.

i scamper about getting my bits
and pieces together; an old lump of york
stone ive been carving gargoils on, based
on my father; plus all the drawings ive
done during the tea breaks.

       *   *   *

springheel sits up front with the driver,
whilst i sit on my own in the back
looking out the window.

i could have been quite happy
on the castle stint, sitting up that
scaffolding, admiring the view. its frank
ile miss most. i carved his name on the
handel of an old walking stick, filled
it with gold paint and gave it to him
as a present. the others all stood back
waighting to see him blow his top.

"he wouldn't of accepted that off
no one but you, gustov." thats ivor
speaking. ron nods in agreement. "if
anybody else had dared give him a walking
stick he'd of belted 'em with it."

chapter 13

2 brothers sit in a kitchen. one, like a
giant cuckoo, is being fed by the wren-
like mother - who darts between the
cooker and the table, bringing 1st toast,
then tea, then eggs and bacon to its
ever open beak. the other sits with a
dry crust on his plate and is making a
drawing.

old nick swills down another
mouthful of tea, then swivels his head to
watch over my shoulder. ive drawn a tea
cup, a teapot, a plate, the edge of the
table, and a hand.

old nick pushes a wedge of butter
into the hot toast, dunks it in a fried
egg and brings it dripping to his mouth.
"you need to draw to the edge of the
page," he advises. "ile give you a
college style tutorial after breakfast,
if you like."

our mother refills his tea cup.

"plus you need to fill-in those
gaps." he points to some spaces on the
picture and takes a swig and pops in
another piece of toast.

"all in all, it would be better to
colour the whole thing in. but better
still, dont draw at all. consentrate on
your ritting. you like ritting, dont you?
im the artist in the family, and one is

enough.

"i can be the son who is an artist
and you can be the son who is the man of
letters.

"but mind what you rite. that stuff
will just get you into trouble. take my
advise - if you can manage that - dont
make the mistake of thinking that what
you rite is the truth, because it isnt.

"as to painting, leave that to me.
you consentrate on your riting. better
still, dont rite either and stick to your
stonemasonry.

"mother tells me that you want to
quit your apprenticship and apply to art
college. take my advise - dont bother.
concentrate on what your good at, which
insidently isnt very much.

"art college would defiantly be a
mistake in your case. listen to someone
whos been there and has a little more
experence of life than you have.

"its not easy to get on in the big
city. and besides, you will always be a
provincial. one would go as far as to
say that you have a predisspostion to
celloquelism.

"okay, when we were younger i
bullied you. i freely admit it. i stamped
on that scooter so's that it would fly up
and hit you in the head. i found it funny
then and i find it funny now. but now its

time to drop all that competertivness and
take some brotherly advise for a change.

"so your thinking of chucking in the
dockyard and going to art skool? its a
good idear. i can give you college style
assessment and tell you where your going
rong. dont look at me like that. thats
your trouble: you cant take advise or
chritisim. you've always been like that.
thats why you wont fit in: your akward
and antagonistic.

"look, ive been around longer than
you have. ive read more books, seen more
films and lived life a little. i could
help you if youd only listen, but you
think you know it all.

"on a seperet subject: i see you've
been wearing a suit. some brotherly
advise: you cant pull it off, you haven't
the posture for it. besides, you know
what your father says 'youve got to have
pernach' well you haven't.

"you remember when we were climbing
that brick pile in nigel formans front
garden and i kicked those bricks down on
top of you? well, you were asking for it.

"draw all you like but you wont get
into art skool, because you haven't got
the verve. stick to your job.

"i couldn't give a fuck about that
stinking backwater. i see myself as not
just living in l -, but as actually
'being of the city!' take my advise, get

out of this shithole whilest you can.
thou of course you wont listen to me."

"thats his problem, he never listens
to anybody." puts in my mother, "you can
tell him till your blue in the face."

"well he needs to bludy listen!"
old nick turns to me "why wont you bludy
listen!"

"because hes just like his soddin
father!" undelines my mother, putting yet
more toast down in front of old nick.

"i dont suppose you want butter
on yours?" my mother asks me. i shake my
head.

"exactly!" shouts my big brother "he
behaves like father, he eats like father
and he looks like him."

"he always was a fussy eater," adds
my mother.

"and he cryed all the time when he
was a baby!" joins in old nick. "egg and
chips and choclet, thats all he'd eat."

old nick smiles in blissfull
contentment. "he's going to get terrible
spots. your just the type to get seveir
achny. look, you've already got spots and
they'er going to get a lot worse.

"youed better get used to being on
your own, because i tell you, no women
will touch you, not with boils.

"yes, youed be best off staying
in the dockyard. the big city is a
complicated place. im not saying you
wouldn't get on, its just what with you
not being able to read and rite. and what
art skool would take you anyway? they
dont like thick-o's you know.

"youed best stay where you are. you
dont like the dockyard? your'll just have
to lump it!"

the devils own anvil

a seeris of indiscriminent hammer blows
resonded thru the fog bound air. if at
1ˢᵗ they seamed sparodic and unrelated
that is because they were, but by and
by it was possible to decern a patten.
in fact they were growing ever sharper
and fervent, every new clout gaining in
urgency, till the hole yard seamed to be
clanging in a feverish creshendo on the
devils own anvil.

bill chucks down his newspaper,
drops his fag butt in his tea and jumps
up.

"christ, look lively, springheel
jacks on the war path! gustov, grab
that hammer and chisel, look lively!
and smudge some dirt on your face, for
chists sake, youve not been on a picnic!
brincat! . . . brincat! . . . brincat!
. . . where the f- is he? . . . there
you are! wake up, get the sleep out of
your eyes and look bissy. on 2ⁿᵈ thorts
youed best just scarper. get under the
pyramid and make yourself scearse!"

brincat sloutches away notchulont
as you like. bill has to give him another
dressing down and finnaly he gets his
bearings and heads for the door. he's

only gone 5 seconds before he rushes back
in with panic in his small eyes.

"its too late, he's here! i almost
walk't rite into him. where shall i hide,
his bound to rumble me!"

the door opens and springheel
bounces in rite behind him, bill just has
time to shuv brincat into the shadows.

i stand whistling and chipping at
my block of stone. i glance up then stoop
to cearfully exinming the surfis with my
finger tips. i put my head to one side
and squint expertly along the serfiss,
brushing off the dust and blowing at a
lump of shale.

springheel looks at me momenterialy
before bill drags him into a bright and
cheerfull converstaion.

"ah, mister brightstone! what a
plesent surprise. i was just planning on
coming over the cabin to run a couple of
numbers past you with my magic pencil."

bill pulls out hes note book and
manovers springheel round the room till
he's got his back to brincat, then
starts scratching down some very rude
calculations. he allows springheel to
lean in and correct him on some very
elimentray mistakes, then makes a sign
with his eyes to brincat over springheels
shoulder.

"so hows the boy shapping up, bill?"

and springheel nods at me.

"fair to middling, mister brightstone. he's bright enough, but you know what today's youngsters are like, drawing this and drawing that."

"dose he aply himself, cubbit, has he got what it takes? . . . and besides all that, is there really any need to train up another mason or is it just a needless expence?"

"im sure he'll be good value for money, mister brightstone, but he does need a set of tools. the lads intiteled by rites."

again bill makes eyes at brincat to go hide. springheel turns to look but brincat ducks back in time.

"what are you about, cubbit?" and springheel swings his head round, "is there someone back there? . . ."

"back there? no, mister brightstone. it must be the dockyard moggy."

"a cat?"

"most likely. but like i say, i cant train the lad without tools, can i, mister brightstone."

"he'll get his tools soon enough. once we get a chit issued. besides, his not indentured yet. we dont want to be splashing out before the inks dryed. theres no point throwing good money after bad."

theres a clang and springheel snaps
his head on his shoulders and peers into
the darkness at the back of the pumping
station. "thats not a cat." springheel
narrows his eyes, "someone's back there,
cubbit."

bill draws himself up. "just a
fitter, mister brightstone, re-primeing
the pump."

"a fitter? well tell him to come
out from behind that infernal machine
so's i can see their face."

bill coughs. "okay son, out
you come. dont be frightend, mister
brightsone wants to see you, thats all."

brincat steps forward, still half
shrowded in shadows.

"come on lad, show yourself. i wont
bite you."

"he's a bit touched, mister
brightstone. its best not to mess with
him."

springheel wrinkles his forehead at
bill. "im sorry?"

bill taps his temple.

and brincat takes the oppertuinty to
sidel off towards the doorway. springheel
clocks him, "hoy! you, come back here!"
brincat pulls up short. "i haven't

finished with you, yet. hold on a minit,
dont i know you from somewhere, take that
bit of rag from infront of your face."

bill sighs, "do as mister
brightstone says, lad. come on now, put
your snot-rag away." and bill launches
into an impassioned speech, "you see,
his my labourer, mister brightstone. his
harmless enough . . . all he wants is . .
."

springheel holds up his hand to
shush bill. "whats that in your lammy,
lad?"

brincat brings up his hand as if to
protect the lump that is moving benieth
the breast of his fearnaught.

"thats furrycat, mister brightstone."
chimes bill.

"who?" and springheel scrunches up
his brow.

"furrycat. its the name of hes
polecat, mister brightstone. its company
for him in the nite."

"he's got a stinking ferrit!"
ejaculates springheel.

"no, its a polecat, mister
brightstone. it dose pong a bit, but the
lads trained it." adds bill, with a hint
of pride.

"i cant belive what im hearing,
cubbit. you know full well his not to

bring pets in here. its against all the regulations. that creature needs to go. how do you know it hasnt got rabbis!"

"its a clean animal, mister brightstone . . . and at the end of the day what are regulations but pieces of paper? theres no harm done after all."

springheel has stopped listening. "you lad, come over here. whats your name?"

"he hasent exactly got a name." mutters bill.

spingheal rounds on bill with a new hostility, "of course hes got a bluddy name, cubitt. now let him speak for himself. boy, show me your pass."

"nor a pass," says bill quietly.

springheel unplugs his ears. "well how else does he get in and out of the gate?"

"he dosnt get in or out," says bill levely, "he lives here."

springheel looks at bill with growing horror. "your not telling me . . . my god, i know who he is, i knew it all along, his one of those escapees!" springheel turns on brincat, "your from the hulks, arnt you!"

"hes a good lad, mister brightstone."

300

springheel now shouts fully in bills
face "your responsible for this, cubitt.
this is another one for horrid hill."

bill and springheel contemplate each
other. i take in both of their profiles,
the old and the young. one with a new
fresh nose on, the other with a great
dirty honker.

theres another clang and we all turn
to see brincat picking up a club hamer.

"you leave him be, you rubber-
kneck!" and brincat steps forward
menacingly.

springheel looks at brincat in utter
amazment, then turns to bill. "do you see
this cubitt? this is the behaviour you've
been encouraging."

bill mearly lowers his head,
touching his thumb and middle finger to
his eye-lids.

"say what you like, no one aint
gonna save you now," spits brincat.

springheel steps backward. "you need
to calm yourself down, lad. your already
in enough trouble as it is. put that
thing down and we can all talk about it
sencibly. but you cant go on living in
the yard! and that ferrit has to go!"

"it aint no fucking ferrit, its a
polecat you cunt!"

"polecat, ferrit, its obvious

that the creature needs to be . . . re-
housed."

brincat draws his arm back and
flings the hamer at springheel, who leaps
into the air in a grand allegro. the
hammer handle strikes springheels shins
then clatters to the floor.

brincat starts circling springheel.

springheel turns to bill with a look
of desperation, "cubbit, say something!"

"theres not a lot i can say, mister
brightstone. the lad loves his polecat."

brincat makes a loung at springheel.
who hops sideways.

"you keep away from me. all of
you are in very serious trouble." and
he waves his finger in the air and even
fixes me a stair.

suddenly brincat stands bolt
uprite and rips his shirt clean off his
own back. the metal buttons ping off,
scurrying to the 4 corners of the pumping
station. "come on then, you big ponce,
do you want some fucking shirts off or
fucking what!"

springheel makes a faint to the left
then dashes for the door. brincat slips
on a patch of oil then takes off after
him. straight away he runs back in, dumps
furrycat, snatches up the hammer and runs
back out.

bill scoops up furrycat and nods at
me to follow brincat. "go keep an eye on
him, gustov. make sure he dosnt get into
any mischief."

as i step outside theres a burst of
sunlite that breaks thru the gray clouds
and illuminates the lock and inner basin.

already brincat is sprinting down
the quay side, waving the hammer like
a tomerhawk. meanwhile springheel is
crossing the 2nd canver, hes feet pounding
over the iron plating. every few strydes
he turns and looks desperately over his
shoulder. brincat vaults the chain guard
and is almost on him.

other faces appear from the
catercombs, a hole raft of site-seers.
one by one they down tools and come to
admire the view.

a cheer goes up as springheel makes
7veral turns round the motorised capstens
with brincat apparently slowing up a
little to add a little drama to a one
sided chase.

they turn and disappear down a
rat run between 2 rusting nissen huts,
then re-apear from behind the gash bins.
theres one last view of them galloping
along between the legs of the great
crains.

even from this distence, its
possible to see springheel stagger, and
one can almost imagin his gasps as he

starts to loos pace. brincat is mearly
playing cat and mouse with him, making
him run on by threats and curses, but not
desiring to actually catch him or he mite
really have to bludgion him to death. and
then there gone.

bill comes up behind me, still
holding furrycat. "well the ponce had it
coming!" and he turns and re-enters the
pumping station.

i stand for a moment looking across
the stretch of glinting water. then a
fresh squall moves in and i follow bill
back inside.

chapter 15

a smashed-up hand

you have to walk down 3 big steps and
then your in the shop.

    it wasn't exactly a basement, but
then again, you couldn't legitmetly
describe it as being on ground level
either. it was as if it was between and
betwixet, but not exactly. it was more on
ground level but kind of sunken.

    and to call it a shop was a stretch.
there is a single boot, apparently on
display in the little window out front,
but you get the feeling that it could
have just as easyerly been left lying
there by accedent. for one thing, you
have to get down on your hands and knees
somewhat to get a clear butchers at it.
theres no doubt that it is a boot, a
left one by the look of it, plus theres
something that could be a price tag laced
thru one of the eye holes. only the tag
is just turned away in such a manner
that no matter how you crook your kneck,
or squint at it, it always remains just
out of reach of your eyes, and you begin
to suspect that is not a price-tag, but
perhaps a dead moth.

    just down those 3 steps and your at
the front door, like you are thigh deep

in concreate, and there, tacked to the
door, is a piece of hard board with the
opening times painted on it: boot shop.
open 12 to 1 wed and thurs only. so i
have come to the rite place after all.

i push open the black painted door
and step into the gloom.

the walls are covered in musturd
coloured paper and theres a row of safty
posters pinned up with various warnings
about loosing your toes in this or that
accident. another poster, stuck below
what passes for a front counter, has
pictures of all different styles of boots
which are suppossidly available.

it would be nice if someone stepped
from the shadows and spoke to me, or a
little bell tinkeled out back, but no,
nothing.

i call out and listen for an answer,
but nothing. i turn to leave. thats when
i notice something to the left, just
inside the door: a werk boot, glued to a
plank of wood.

this little mystry is hidden from
view when you 1st come in, but now it
presents itself. this werk boot has
been sawn down the middle, expossing a
layer of steal that has been crafterly
sandwiched in the toecap. the leather
either side of this saw cut is all
raggedy, so its possible to pick bits
off.

just then a tall fellow, with a hook
neck looms out of nowhere.

"you leave that display alone!"

and he rests his over sized hands on
the counter and hunches up his shoulders
at me.

"i was just feeling how thick the
metal was."

"its thick enough. its for looking
at, not playing with."

"its a nice shop you've got here," i
venture, squinting up at the strip lite.

"very nice im sure. now what do you
want, ive not got all day," and he pulls
out an ancent pocket watch on a black
morning chain and studies it. "hurry up,
my dinners getting cold."

"i was just admiring your poster. do
you have all of those boots."

he drops his pocket watch back
into his waistcoat pocket. "yes, we stock
most sizes and styles. those we dont have
i can order in. it takes 2 weeks, under
normal circumstances."

i look at the mans nose and deside
what to say next. "i was just wondering,
ive heard that you stock the exacutive
range?"

"as i said, we stock most sizes, up
to 13. would you like some boots?"

"i was thinking more along the line of shoes."

"for yourself?" i nod, "becouse we dont allow people to buy footwear for those on the outside, who dont werk here. it wouldn't be fair, would it?"

"i suppose not," i say doubtfully.

"thats the whole point of the yard discount."

"yes, i can see your point."

"so these are for you?"

"yes, theyer for me."

"and you are? . . ."

"gustov."

"not your name, im not your boy friend, whats your trade?"

"im a stonemason. apprentice."

"with the psa?"

"yes."

"so your'll be wanting our standard thunder boot, then."

"what colours do they come in?"

"what do you mean 'what colours do they come in?' pink with purple spots! black is the colour they come in. standared black. what size?"

"like i was saying, im more
interested in the shoes."

"shoes are for management only.
you'd be better suited with a boot. the
ones on the left are the cheapist." and
he extends one of his long arms, which
stretches clear across the counter and in
front, his huge hand elegantly scrolling
down the illustrations on the poster
below.

thou in its self monsterious, the
hand still travels slowly and all in all
exhibits a suprizing amount of grace.

i look at the poster but cant really
focus on what he is trying to flog me on
account of being mesmerized by his giant
fingernails.

i shake my head and look away. "do
you have any winkle pickers? you know,
like those punk rockers wear."

"punk rockers?"

"teddy boys, then."

hookneck holds me with a cold stare.

"i dont hold with teddy boys, mods
or skin heads. what you see is what we've
got."

i point to the picture of the
executive brogue.

"what about those?"

hookneck juts his torso over the counter and peers over the edge.

"as i have already made clear to the young sir, those are management shoes. a bricky will be wearing thunder boots!"

"but im not a bricky."

he looks at me doubtfully. everthing about his expression declairs that he takes me for a lier.

"if your not a bricky then what are you?"

"i told you, im a stonemasons apprentice."

"a stonemasons apprentice, really?" he see's that im serroius, "well i cant be expected to remember everything can i. so what colour boots?"

"i like the patten on the toecaps of these shoes."

hookneck shakes his head. "no, no, no, tecknicly thats a brogue not a shoe. besides, you need ankle protection, and that particular style would cost you more than a weeks wadges."

i stroke my chin, staring hard at the picture.

"a weeks wages. really?"

"£16.99, those buties are. now stop waisting my time, these werk boots

are our standard," and he points at a
riddiclious pair of black coffins with
inflated toecaps, "steal toe caps, and
acid resistant souls. £4.50, all in."

"they look pretty rubbish to me."

hookneck sucks his teeth and draws
his shoulders up towards the cealling. i
decide to rephrase my assesment.

"obviousely they are excillent value
for money, its just that i was looking
for something a bit more on the semi-
smart side."

"your not going to the opera, you
werk in the dockyard."

"never-the-less, i would like to
purches a pair, please."

"the executive is our flag ship
model. ive told the young sir that he
cant afford those shoes. they'er top of
line, not for apprentice stonemasons or
the like."

i pull out 2 10 pound notes and
place them on the werk bench.

hook neck survays the notes with
disdain.

"size?"

"8's, please."

and he turns and heads out back,
muttering.

i here him rummaging about out there, throwing about empty boxes by the sounds of it.

"size 8, size 8, size 8."

finnaly he comes back looking quite pleased with himself.

"im afraid the young sir is out of luck, we'er out of 8's."

"could you put them on order for me?"

"ordinarily yes, but ive had the executive on back order for 3 months or more. theres problems procuring the pebble grained leather, so were not taking any more orders on that line. thats the way it is now days, everything's coming to an end."

and he smiles at me, evidently very pleased with the fact.

"do you have them in a 9?"

"the young sir wants to make he's mind up. are you an 8 or a 9?"

"usually im an 8, but im still growing and i thort i could try a 9."

"the executive come up a bit on the large size, a 9 would fit more like a 10."

"thats alrite, im a large 8. really i should take a 9. besides its best to leave room to grow."

hookneck snorts, turns and goes
out back. theres the sound of a small
avalarunch, then he comes back in and
flings a box down on the counter in front
of me.

"9's! but i cant see theyle be much
good to you."

i see the shoes peeping out at me
from the white tissue paper, like 2 dark
lumps of mahogany.

theres a small stool provided and
i sit and try them on. on the whole they
apear to fit very well. i stand and try
walking across the room. despite their
eligent profile the shoes are deceptively
heavy and i can feel the heels slipping
on and off with every step.

"too big?" asks hookneck, hopfully.

"no, on the contary, theyer a little
on the snug side, im wondering if i
should try a 10."

"we've no 10's." says hookneck,
levely.

"actually, on 2nd thorts these are
perfict. i think ile leave them on. can
you chuck these in your bin." and i hand
him bills old football boots.

❋   ❋   ❋

as i walk back across to the bulls
nose i feel peoples eyes on me. it is
as if these good, fine, honest werkers
instintivly know what is about to happen;
what destiny has in store for me, that i
am bound for greatness.

and even if some brains are slower
than others and do not already see
greatness enscribed there on my forhead,
then certenly they are at least awear of
my brand new shoes, of my confident step.

naturally they still have steal
toecaps. the very waight of the shoes
carrys me forward, like swinging
pendulums. but rather than the apperence
of great clod-hoppers they have been
cunningly made in the brogue style.

is that why their eyes follow
my every step as i prance round this
dockyard of theirs? yes, that im cut from
a different cloth than a regular bricky,
is obvious even to the untrained eye.
indeed, that is why brincat scowls at me:
for i have been to the dockyard boot shop
and successfully purchessed a pair of
middle management safty foot wear.

and after the dockyard?

of course my mother is dead set on
my staying in this birth for life. the
dockyard was good enough for granddad
lewis. do i think that i am better than
him? and even my fathers father was in
the dockyard after he retired from the
royal navi. and great grandfather william

too, and another one befor him, whos
name i dont know. yes, the dockyard is
something of a tradition in my family,
and tradition isn't to be sneezed at, or
mocked by aspiring poets.

for hevens sake, why is it always
'dockyard this' and dockyard that? people
get caught up with phrases and fixate
on words when there really is no need.
is there no other word in the english
language than dockyard! and rather than
'dockyard' why not just use plain languge
and simply call it a prison hulk?

for sure we are each others
geaolers, whatching each others every
move; keeping a weather eye in case one
of us should wake from this dream and
make a break for it. after all, prisoners
oft make the best gaolers in the world.

       ✻   ✻   ✻

i curl my toes to help hold my shoes on,
and notchelently stroll into the pumping
station.

bill looks up from his sandwich. "so
you've got new shoes."

"oh these?" and look down at my
feet, and faign indifference, "i thort
thyed keep me going for the time being."

"i hope you've still got my football

boots."

"yes."

"good. ile be wanting those back."

i walk over to my block of stone and scrutinize it.

"i bet they cost a pretty penny."

"no, they were reduced. theyer not making them anymore."

"you wont be wanting to wear those in front of springheel, yourll just antagonize him. and wheres the point in that?"

i get my sketch book out and walk round my cube of stone and start drawing it.

"if you take those back rite away theres a chance they'll give you your money back. are you sure they fit?"

"yes."

"they look a bit loose."

"the man said thats how they'er ment to be. besides, he said i need to wear 2 pairs of socks. is it alright if i draw you?"

"draw away. but i want no more talk of chucking your apprenticship in. you cant make a living from drawing. what you gonna do, chop your bleeding ear off."

i chew on my toung, effortlessly
scetching bills missrable portrate. as
far as noses go, bill's isn't a minow.

"do your drawing in your spair time.
picture making? its a hobby. this is a
real job and real job has security." and
he looks around the pumping station, as
if trying to convince himself.

"get your apprentiship under
your belt and you buy yourself all the
coloured pencils you want. only someone
with sawdust between their ears would
chuck the dockyard in for poncing around
in a berrit!"

is it really that bills eyes are
that tiny, or is it that they just aprear
that way when laid along side that
breezer of his.

bill sips his tea, crumbles a bit of
nibby and feeds a little face that comes
peeping out the top of his top pocket. i
see rite away that its furrycat.

"i thort i smelled something."

"well you were rite."

i put my pencil down and look about.
i knew something was different.

"where is brincat?"

"gone! old springheel had him
took by the merines. they carted him off
back to the hulks. left me to look after
furrycat."

"i thort you didnt like him stinking
up the place."

"dead cert i dont, but somebody's
got to feed the poor little bleeder.
besides ile take it ferreting this
weekend, my old mrs cooks up a lovely
rabbit pie. no, if he pays his way he
stays."

bill lifts furycat in the air,
squirming like a fur snake. "but if
you bite my finger, ile drown you, you
bugger!"

      ✻   ✻   ✻

the weather dosn't exactly get along with
bill's health, great northern blasts,
showers of hail and sleet. he comes in
the mornings and just sits there, blowing
on his mitts.

"the quack told me quit smoking and
take a holiday. oh yeah, and what on, my
push bike? steer clear of the damp, he
says, and what hope is there of that,
we're virtually in the bludy river!

"springheel was in here giving me
an ear-full. 1st they drag off my labourer
and now their crying that the caisson
needs to be functioning by the 1st of the
month. apparently we'er holding up the
entire bleeding navi. but whats the point

of going out on site in this weather?"

   it is still just about possible
for me to sit in the caboos and imagine
my werking life stretching into a
distent point in time. but what happens
to a young artists hart and soul in
such cases? to hear the sounds of life
whistling past ones ears and know that
the final days are approaching and
meanwhile your star has dimmed.

   bill flips the lid on his backy
tin and dips in his fat fingers, wide,
yet dainty. a few strands of tobacco. he
sticks out a gray looking toung and licks
at the paper: a perfect roll-up.

   "theres no point you being stuck
out in upnor. whats springheel want to go
and send you out to the back of bleeding
beyond for? thats what i ask myself. as
if i cant teach all you need to know. i
aint pushing up daisys, yet!"

   bill flicks a match, drags down
a lungful and lets it trickle out in
wisps of blue-grey. he bites at the air
and makes a perfict smoke ring. i watch
mesmerised, caught in time, my chin at
an angle. then bill bangs his chest,
has a coughing fit and spits into his
handkichief.

   "youed best go out on your own
today. i cant go out there. in this
weather? it will kill me! besides, ive
still got to get my ticket from the
sugery.

"remember all that ive taught you,
youre a craftsman, not a demolition
party! and dont use the machines, you'll
have to do it by hand. you cant use that
kit unless your supervised. keep your
set-square handy. i'd come with you, only
my hart." he bangs on his chest again and
hic-ups up a little oyster, just to prove
he's not sloping shoulders.

"get some fire under your arse,
springheel will be in here before you
know it. and pass me my tool-wrap. its in
my donky box."

i go fetch it, and place it in
front of him. bill pulls on the strings,
unrolls it on the bench, smoothes out the
4 corners, then extracts something heavy
from the deepest pocket. he waighs it
in his hand and passes it to me; burred
edges, grey metal.

"my master, samauel ketch gave me
this granit smasher. his master gave it
to him, and now im passing it to you: my
club hammer, the big boy, four pound."

"but what about my tool's, mister
cubitt?"

"here, ive told you, none of that
mister stuff. im bill."

i nod. "when am i going to get my
tools, bill?"

"there arnt going to be any tools,
gustov. they've stiched you up like a

320

kipper. the hole things harry taters,
from start to finish - no one gives a
damn anymore - its all breeze blocks and
precast concreat now days. masonrys a
dead craft, lad."

"but they said . . ."

"they said, they said! fuck
'em! pardon my french. there all in
it together: the boss's, the bankers
- they'er all cunts! no one cears for
skill and buti anymore. they've given up
the fight, even the werking man. all they
cear about is their dicks and ackers.

"here, help yourself to some
tickler." bill passes his tobbaco pouch.
"roll yourself one, go on, i know you've
been watching me. no, like this, thumb
and forefinger . . . thats more like it .
. . but heres the tricky bit, folding it
back on itself. you've got to catch the
edge, and mind you dont drop none . . .
thats the ticket, now lick it! ah, now
thats an easy mistake to make . . . look,
no, turn it round, you see the glue?
its on the other side, you've rolled it
backwards. never mind its easily done.
here take mine," and bill sparks it up
for me. i taste it: hot and bitter.

"dont play with it! go on, take it
down, youre not a girl are you? i thort
you were a pipe smoker!"

i grin through the tears. i try to
hold my cough, i take a deep puff. bill
encourages me with his eyes.

"thats it, thats it, take it all
down! we'll make a mason of you yet!

"if the barometer rises, ile be
out there and help you. but in this pea
souper? in my condition? its not on, is
it? ile give you my hammer and you can
use as many of the pnumatic points as you
like, only by hand, mind. you with me?
use your nod. have respect for yourself
and your craft, a noble craft, no bricky,
no labourer, a stonemason! a dying art,
but an ancent one! from rameses to the
acropolis, from the coliseum to the
cenotaph - from bill cubbit to you,
gustov, lad.

"like i say, if this pea souper
lifts ile be out there like a shot .
. . meanwhile you know where i am if
you need me, ile be right here . . . i
fancy a little buttered toast and maybe
some beans in tomato sauce . . . right,
off you go now and dont let springheel
catch you swinging the lead! ile hold up
in here. heres some tickler for later,
tomorrow you buy your own!"

*   *   *

i have a last glymps into the warm
cosyness: a shed from a different era,
not done up since the 1940s. steaming
mugs of tea and damaged faces woofing
toast and marge.

"shut that bluddy door, you cows
son!"

        and the door bangs shut and im alone
in the world.

        i walk out and let the door bang
behind me. its still foggy out. rolling
in off the river.

        you can just make out a row of
derricks and then some funnels drifting
in and out of the swirls. small figurs
hurry by and disappear for good.

        i take a few lugs on the foul
tasting snout, then ditch it in the
oggin.

        bills bike is lent up against the
wall so i climb on and cycle out into
that fog: animal-like, trundling down in
great waves, fathoms thick . . . it wraps
you up.

                ✳   ✳   ✳

bill sending me out like that in to the
cold air with nothing but a lump hammer?
i button my collar, and shiver in that
other world . . . and no tools to speak
off either, just pnumatic points with
no striking surfiss. the end you hit is
narrower than the shaft. and the castings
are so brittle they just shatter when you
belt them with the hammer.

                        323

and that granite, a little on the robust side? 1000ths of an inch to be taken off across the entire surfis area. expanding, blue-grey, with a grainy finish, more like metal than rock. 2 and a 1/2 foot across, recessed in a little sump hole - so's you have to get down on your stomach, lean your head and shoulders into the pit, then try to hit the point.

i chew on my tongue, raise the hammer to my shoulder and bring it down on the point with a mighty wollop. theres a blinding flash - the scene's illuminated in a shower of sparks; they fizz off like fire werks, some findig my eyes. when my vision clears i look down at my hand which has been pepped with tiny flecks of scrappnel. i wipe the blud off. and no safety specks either.

i try another couple of hits, trying to get the point into the hidden corners, where theres a couple of bits of rough stuff sticking up.

the hammer slips, once, twice. i lose my grip. my hand is numbed by the cold and the reverberations. i claw my fingers . . . a dull feeling, little bits of electricity.

no one is saying that the job set before me is pointless, and in all likely hood, somewhere in the world there exists a more taxing and impossible task. but is it really fair to lay the entire futcher

of the comings and goings of the royel
navi on the narrow shoulders of a 16
year old apprentice, lieing on his tummy
beside a fogbound sea-lock with his head
stuck down a 2 foot pit?

i pull myself up and examin my
hand. i dab away the blud and you can
actually see little shards of metal under
the skin. also, the hammer has left
7veral bruces where it has slipped off
the narrow sriking surfis. then i look
down and notice that the toe caps of my
excutive broughs have been badly scuffed
from crawling about on my tummy.

in sudden rage i raise the hammer
and bring it down on my hand, 1,2,3,4,5
times in quick succssession . . . theres
a sickening thud, and the hammer bounces
as it hits the flesh. i cry out and sit
rocking back and forth on the ground,
cradling my poor, dumb stupid hand.

ugly, sinful hand! unlovable and
bad hand that will never hold a woman!
i get to my knees, grit my teeth, then
raise the hammer and smash it down once
more, and again and again. at 1st lightly,
then gaining power. this time i let out a
little scream and fling the hammer away
from me, so's it skids across quay side
and drops into the oggin.

one second im lying there,
swallowing the fog, and the next,
everything goes in flashes. my hand pokes
from my tattered sleeve, bluded and

shattered. i draw it up to my breast,
take my scarf and wrap it, precious, a
fold, delicate, i warm it . . . and my
butiful new shoes are scuffed and ruined.

i teach myself a lesson! i show my
hand what for! i let it know who's boss.

i stumble off, limping on account of
my new shoes. the truth is they pinch a
little. instantly i can feel them wearing
a blister.

in all honesty, who would wear such
a pair of preposterious, over-priced
shoes, but a vile climber. a traitor to
his class and his artistic creed.

i sit down on the wheel benieth
one of the great crains and ease these
hiddious boss's shoes off. my toes
stretch out on the cold cobbles, so happy
to at last taste freedom. the stink of
new leather - hot and pungent - rises and
attacks my nostrels.

to be pefictly frank these super
fine shoes are not nearly as eligent as
they at 1st promised. it is one thing to
conjour up dreams via a colour picture
in a glossy catolouge, but quite another
to experence the harsh reality of a pair
of ill-fitting coffins. the inner soles
arn't soft and lusorious, as one mite
expect, but in point of fact are lumpy
with hidden nails.

just take a look at the word
'exsecutive' embossed there in gold. what

rubbish! no, ive been sold a pair of
duds. rather than being a pair of fine,
eligent, brogues these shoes are stinking
class trators fit only for the scrap
heap.

i turn and look about me but no ones
watchin me. still cradling my damaged
hand, i hobble over to the edge of the
basin, peer into the oily waters bellow
and drop my left shoe. it hits the surfis
with a muffeld splash and actually sails
off across the basin.

i hold out the rite shoe at arms
length and also let it go. there is a 2nd
muffeld splash and this one imediately
capsizes and sinks benieth the black
waves.

so i turn and limp off bare footed,
picking my way thru the cobbels, towards
the main gate.

apprentice stonemason,
the bulls-nose, c- dockyard, 1976

about the author

billy chyldish is an extraordinary and
prolific artist of international repute.
smart and good looking, his creative
practice spans many media including
painting, writing and music. he currently
lives - and works - in c - , north k -,
with his wife and daughter. chyldish
continues to exhibit his work around the
world. this is his 5th novel, the others
being:

my fault

notebooks of a naked youth

sex crimes of the futcher

the idiocy of idears